BARON MUNCHAUSEN
and other Comic Tales from Germany

A noble stag . . . with a fine full-grown cherry tree between his antlers. (See page 7)

BARON MUNCHAUSEN
and other Comic Tales
from Germany

by R. E. Raspe and Others

Edited by

STELLA HUMPHRIES

Illustrated by

ULRIK SCHRAMM

LONDON: J. M. DENT & SONS LTD
NEW YORK: E. P. DUTTON & CO. INC.

RUDOLF ERICH RASPE (1737–94) was born in Hanover, Germany, and studied at Göttingen University. Scientist, literary critic and antiquarian, he was appointed curator of Cassel Museum in 1767. Unfortunately he embezzled coins from the collection to pay his private debts, and he had to flee the country to escape imprisonment.

In 1775 he settled in England, still dogged by disgrace and debts. He lived precariously on the proceeds of his journalism and his antiquarian and scientific enterprises. It was whilst the 'queer Mr Raspe' was working for Matthew Boulton, James Watt's partner, in the Cornish tin mines, that he published the adventures of Baron Munchausen in 1785. In 1794 Raspe died of scarlet fever in Ireland.

There was a real Baron Munchausen, a fellow countryman of Raspe's, who was well known in his day as a genial host and a raconteur. However, his name would have been forgotten long ago had not Raspe immortalized him as 'the Prince of Liars'. The original tales have been added to by many authors, and the best of these later additions, with the old spellings and punctuation, are included in this volume, which explains the 'Raspe and others' of the title-page.

'The Schildburgers' (here called 'The Men of Schilda'), first published anonymously in 1597, is a collection of folk tales about a community of simpletons. It has parallels in the literature of many countries from Iceland to Japan, including an English version known as the 'Wise Men of Gotham'.

In this volume the character of 'Till Eulenspiegel' has been added to the original. His adventures were first printed, also anonymously, about 1478, and described the wanderings of a rogue and vagabond, who teased and bluffed his way across central Europe, living on his wits.

S. H.

First published in this edition in Great Britain, 1971.

ISBN: 0 460 05096 6

CONTENTS

MUNCHAUSEN

THE MEN OF SCHILDA

Translated and abridged by Stella Humphries

The first seven stories are translated from a retelling by Georg Paysen Petersen and used here by kind permission of Loewes Verlag, Bayreuth.

The last three stories have been freely translated from 'Volksbuecher', Vol. I, 'Die Schildbürger', retold by G. O. Marbach published Otto Wigan, Leipzig, 1838.

ILLUSTRATIONS

COLOUR

BLACK AND WHITE

ix

TO THE PUBLIC

Having heard, for the first time, that my adventures have been doubted, and looked upon as jokes, I feel bound to come forward and vindicate my character *for veracity*, by paying three shillings at the Mansion House of this great city for the affidavits hereto appended.

This I have been forced into in regard of my own honour, although I have retired for many years from public and private life; and I hope that this, my last edition, will place me in a proper light with my readers.

AT THE CITY OF LONDON, ENGLAND
We, the undersigned, as true believers in the *profit*, do most solemnly affirm, that all the adventures of our friend Baron Munchausen, in whatever country they may *lie*, are positive and simple facts. *And*, as we have been believed, whose adventures are tenfold more wonderful, *so* do we hope all true believers will give him their full faith and credence.

GULLIVER	X
SINBAD	X
ALADDIN	X

Sworn at the Mansion House
9th Nov. last in the absence
of the Lord Mayor.
JOHN (*the Porter*).

CHAPTER ONE

I set off from home on my journey to Russia to join the Imperial Army then at war with the Turks. It was in the midst of winter for I had a just notion that frost and snow must of course mend the roads, which every traveller had described as uncommonly bad through the northern parts of Germany, Poland, Courland, and Livonia. I went on horseback, which is the most convenient manner of travelling. I was but lightly clothed, of this, I felt the inconvenience, the more I advanced north-east. What must not a poor old man have suffered in that severe weather and climate, whom I saw on a bleak common, in Poland, lying on the road, helpless, shivering, and hardly having wherewithal to cover his nakedness.

I pitied the poor soul. Though I felt exceedingly cold myself, I threw my mantle over him and immediately I heard a voice from the heavens, blessing me for that piece of charity, saying:

'I'll be damned my son if I do not reward it in time.'

I went on: night and darkness overtook me. No village was to be seen. The country was covered with snow, and I was unacquainted with the road.

Tired, I alighted at last, and fastened my horse to something of a pointed stump of a tree which appeared above the snow. For the sake of safety I took my pistols under my arm, and lay down in the snow, not far off, where I slept so soundly, that I did not open my eyes till it was full daylight. Great was my astonishment now, to find myself in the midst of a village, lying in the churchyard. Nor was my horse to be seen, but I heard him soon after neigh, somewhere above me. On looking upwards I beheld him tied and hanging to the weather-cock of the steeple. Matters were now very plain to me: The village had been covered with snow that night; a sudden change of weather had taken place; I had sunk down to the churchyard whilst asleep, gently, and in the same proportion as the snow had melted away, and what in the dark I had taken to be a stump of a little tree appearing above the snow, to which I had tied my horse, proved to have been the cross or weather-cock of the steeple.

Without long consideration I took one of my pistols, shot off the halter, brought down the horse and proceeded on my journey.

On passing through Warsaw, I made the acquaintance of an elderly general who had lost part of his skull during an engagement with the Turks. However, he had had a silver plate fitted as a substitute, which was hinged to his cranium, and thus formed a sort of flap. He and I used to meet every day in a certain tavern, where there was much hard tippling.

Presently I became aware of a strange fact. While the rest of us sat there with our faces getting hotter and redder as we imbibed more and more of the strong Tokay, the old gentleman merely ran his fingers through his hair every now and then, and immediately afterwards he appeared perfectly cool and sober. The others present agreed that this was so, and they explained that from time to time, the general would raise his silver plate and allow all the fumes of the wine to escape, so clearing his head.

In order to convince myself that this was indeed the case, I placed myself as it were casually beside the general, with a burning taper in my hand, as if to light my pipe. But instead, I placed the spill close by his head from which the alcoholic fumes were then escaping, and behold, they burnt at once with a most beautiful blue flame. The general who had witnessed my manœuvres, gave me a most beatific smile, like St Nicholas himself, complete with flaming halo.

I was so impressed with this arrangement that I consulted a very skilful goldsmith to discover whether I, too, could obtain such a useful contrivance. He declared that I could, if I were prepared to undergo a trepanning operation, that is for the removal of a portion of my cranium. Or else I could manage to lose such a piece under fire during my next campaign. But so far, neither of these has come about and I am still waiting in vain to acquire this most useful form of ventilation.

My horse carried me well—yet advancing into Russia, where travelling on horseback is rather unfashionable in winter, I submitted, as I always do, to the custom of the country, took a single horse sledge, and drove briskly on towards St Petersburgh. All at once, in the midst of a dreary forest, I spied a terrible wolf making after me, with all the speed of ravenous winter hunger. He soon overtook me. There was no possibility of escape. Mechanically I laid myself down flat in the sledge, and let my horse run for our safety.

What I apprehended, and hardly hoped or expected, happened immediately after. The wolf did not mind me in the least, but took a leap over me, and falling furiously on the horse, began instantly to tear and devour the hind part of the poor animal, which ran the faster for his pain and terror. Thus unnoticed and safe myself, I lifted my head slily up, and with horror I beheld that the wolf ate and broke his way into the horse's body. It was not long before he had fairly forced himself into it; then I took my advantage, fell upon him with the butt end of my whip. This unexpected attack in his rear frightened him much. He leapt forward with all his might; the horse's carcase dropped to the ground; but in his place the wolf was in the harness, and I, on my part whipping him continually, we both arrived, in full career, safe at St Petersburgh, contrary to our respective expectations, and very much to the astonishment of the beholders.

CHAPTER TWO

In Russia, I found myself at leisure for a while, until I received my commission as a company officer. I had no difficulty in filling in the time, however, with all the pleasures of the chase, and one morning I saw through the windows of my bedroom, that a large pond, not far off was, as it were, covered with wild ducks. In an instant I took my gun from the corner, run downstairs, and out in such a hurry, that imprudently I struck my face against the door post. So great was the impact that fire, light and sparks, flew out of my eyes, but it did not prevent my intention. I soon came within shot, when levelling my piece, I observed to my sorrow, that the flint had sprung from the cock, by the violence of the shock I had just received. There was no time to be lost. I instantly remembered the effect it had had upon my eyes, therefore opened the pan, levelled my piece against the wild fowls, and my fist against one of my eyes. A hearty blow drew sparks again, the shot went off, and I had five brace of ducks, four widgeons and a couple of teals.

Chance and good luck often correct our mistakes: of this I had a singular instance soon after, when in the depth of a forest I saw a wild pig and sow running close behind each other. My ball had missed them, yet the foremost pig only ran away, and the sow stood motionless as fixed to the ground. On examining into the matter I found the latter one to be an old sow, blind with age, which had taken hold of her pig's tail, in order to be led along by filial duty. My ball having passed between the two, had cut this leading string, of which the old sow was still chewing the remainder; and as her former guide did not draw her on any longer, she had stopped of course. I therefore laid hold of the remaining end of the pig's tail, and led the old beast home without any further trouble on my part, and without any reluctance or apprehension on the part of the helpless old animal.

Terrible these wild sows are, but more fierce and dangerous are the boars, one of which I had once the misfortune to meet in a forest unprepared for attack or defence. I retired behind an oak tree, just when the furious animal levelled a side cut at me, with such force, that his tusks pierced through the tree, by which means he could neither repeat the blow nor retire. Ho! ho! thought I, I shall soon have you now, and immediately I laid hold of a stone, wherewith I hammered and bent his tusks in such a manner that he could not retreat at all, and must wait my return from the next village, whither I went for ropes and a cart, to secure him properly, and to carry him off safe and alive, which perfectly succeeded.

You have heard, I dare say, of the hunters and sportsman's saint and protector, Saint Hubert; and of the noble stag, which appeared to him in the forest, with the holy cross between his antlers. I hardly know whether there are not such crossed stags even at this present day. But let me rather tell what I have seen myself. Having one day spent all my shot, I found myself unexpectedly in the presence of a stately stag, looking at me so unconcernedly, as if he had known of my empty pouches. I charged immediately with powder, and upon it a good handful of cherries, of which I

There, amid the slumping sacks, stood the frantic bear. (See page 17)

had partly sucked the flesh as far as the hurry would permit. Thus I let fly at him, and hit him just on the middle of the forehead, between his antlers. It stunned him—he staggered —yet he made off. A year or two after I was with a party in the same forest—and behold a noble stag comes out with a fine full-grown cherry tree between his antlers. I recollected my former adventure; looked upon him as my property; and brought him to the ground by one shot, which at once gave me the haunch and cherry sauce; for the tree was covered with the richest fruit, the like I never had tasted before. Many a time since then have I found myself in such a trying situation. There is a kind of fatality in it. The fiercest and most dangerous animals, generally come upon me when defenceless, as if they had a notion or foresight of it by way of instinct.

What do you say of this for example? Daylight and powder were spent one day in a Polish forest. When I was going home, a terrible bear made up to me in great speed, with open mouth ready to fall upon me, all my pockets were searched in an instant for powder and ball, but in vain—I found nothing but two spare flints; one I flung with all my might into the monster's open jaws, down his throat. It gave him pain, and made him turn about, so that I could level the second at his back-door, which, indeed, I did with wonderful success, for it flew in, met the first flint in the stomach, struck fire, and blew up the bear with a terrible explosion. Though I came safe off that time, yet I should not wish to try it again, or venture against bears with no other defence.

Thus too, another time, a frightful wolf rushed upon me so suddenly, and so close that I could do nothing but follow mechanical instinct, and thrust my fist into his open mouth, For safety's sake I pushed on and on, till my arm was fairly in, up to the shoulder. How should I disengage myself? I was not much pleased with my awkward situation. With a wolf face to face, our ogling was not of the most pleasant kind. If I withdrew my arm, then the animal would fly the more furiously upon me; that, I saw in his flaming eyes. In short, I laid hold of his entrails, turned him inside out like a glove and flung him to the ground, where I left him.

CHAPTER THREE

All my narrow and lucky escapes were chances turned to advantage by presence of mind and vigorous exertions; but a man would be a very blameable and imprudent sportsman, who would always depend upon chance and his stars, without troubling to provide himself with the most excellent horses, dogs, guns and swords he can obtain. I have always been remarkable for the quality of my weapons and my animals, as also for the proper manner of using and managing them.

I shall not enter here into any detail of my stables, kennel or armoury, but a favourite dog of mine I cannot help mentioning. It was a greyhound. I never had or saw a better one. He grew old in my service, and was not remarkable for his size but the rather for his uncommon swiftness. I always coursed with him. He ran so fast, so much, and so long in my service, that he actually ran off his legs, so that in the latter part of his life, I was under the necessity of working and using him as a dachshund, in which quality he still served me many years.

I remember too, with pleasure and tenderness, a superb Lithuanian horse, Ajax, which no money could have bought. He became mine by an accident, which gave me an opportunity of showing my horsemanship to a great advantage. I was at Count Przobofsky's noble country seat in Lithuania, and remained with the ladies at tea, in the drawing-room, while the gentlemen were down in the yard, to see a young horse of blood, which was just arrived from the stud. At once we heard a noise of distress—I hastened downstairs, and found the horse so unruly that nobody durst approach or mount him. The most resolute horsemen stood dismayed and aghast. In one leap, I was on his back, frightened him by surprise, and worked him quite into gentleness and obedience, with the best display of horsemanship I was master of. Fully to show this to the ladies, and save them unnecessary trouble, I forced him to leap in at one of the open windows of the tea-room, walked round several times, pace, trot, and gallop; and at last made him mount the tea-table, there to repeat his lessons in a pretty style of miniature, which was exceedingly pleasing to the ladies, for he performed them amazingly well, and did not break either cup or saucer. It put me so high in the opinion of the ladies, and so well in that of the noble lord, that with his usual politeness he begged I would accept of this young horse, and ride him full career to conquest and honour, in the campaign against the Turks, which was soon to be opened, under the command of Count Munich.

I could not indeed have received a more agreeable present. A horse so gentle, so spirited, and so fierce—at once a lamb and a Bucephalus, put me always in mind of the soldier's and the gentleman's duty, of young Alexander and of the astonishing things he performed in the field.

Before we took the field, however, I had one remarkable adventure that ought not to be forgotten. I was riding home one evening after a fair day's sport. The sun was setting and I must have dozed in the saddle, neglecting to give my proper attention to the way ahead. For of a sudden, I was jolted out of my musings or half slumber—call it what you will—as my gallant Ajax pulled up in fright and I saw, stretching immediately before me, a broad strip of black mire. It seemed as if the path petered out completely, only to resume its course on the far side of the morass. Then I recalled some recent talk of a bridge washed away in a thunderstorm and not yet replaced.

Meanwhile, how was I to get home? Should I retrace my steps and seek another way? Unworthy thought! Without a moment's hesitation I dug in my spurs and urged on my steed. Brave Ajax reared and we went soaring into the air. Then it flashed through my mind that after the day's exertions—we had set up above five and twenty hares and caught them all, in the end I lost count there were so many—my horse must be unusually fatigued. In short, he was hardly in good enough trim to make such a prodigious bound without a fair run up. With swift decision I spun him round in mid air, so that he returned at once to the very spot from which he had attempted his heroic leap.

So far so good. I patted the beast's neck, then walked him back a short distance to make another venture. At the right moment I gave him spurs and bit and the horse sailed into the air for the second time.

The miry stretch was, in my estimation, about twenty paces wide, but I quickly recognized that I had misjudged the distance by no less than six paces. Once again I applied the spurs, and Ajax responded with another access of speed. Alas, his spurt was in vain. We could not reach the farther bank, and horse and rider landed together in the squelching morass. The yielding mud had already covered my hips, so that only my torso and the horse's neck and head still showed above the mire. In such a desperate situation something had to be done and fast. Gripping my noble steed tightly between my thighs and grasping my pigtail firmly in my right hand, I gave it such a powerful tug that I hoisted myself and my horse clean out of the swamp and we landed safely on firm ground. Then we set off for home at an easy trot, none the worse for our slight mishap.

CHAPTER FOUR

Modesty forbids individuals to arrogate to themselves great successes or victories, and so I do not claim any particular share of glory in the noble campaign on the River Pruth. We all did our duty, which, in the patriot's, soldier's and gentleman's language, is a very comprehensive word of great honour.

However, having had the command of a body of hussars, I can say that they were brave fellows, all of whom I led to conquest and to victory. We had very hot work once in the van of the army, when we drove the Turks into Oczakow. My spirited Ajax had almost brought me into a scrape. I had an advanced forepost, and saw the enemy coming against me in a cloud of dust, which left me rather uncertain about their actual numbers and real intentions. To wrap myself up in a similar cloud of dust was common prudence, or answered the end for which I had been sent out. Therefore I let my flankers on both wings spread to the right and left and make what dust they could, and I myself led on straight upon the enemy, to have a nearer sight of them; and that I had, for they stood and fought, till for fear of my flankers, they began to move off rather disorderly. This was the moment to fall upon them with spirit—— We broke them entirely, made a terrible havoc amongst them—and drove them not only back

to a walled town in their rear, but even through it, contrary
to our most sanguine expectation.

By reason of the swiftness of my Lithuanian I had been
foremost in the pursuit; and seeing the enemy fairly flying
through the opposite gate, I thought it would be prudent to
stop in the market-place to order the trumpet to rendezvous.
I stopped, but judge of my astonishment, when in this
market-place I saw neither trumpet nor any living body of
my hussars about me. Are they scouring the other streets, I
wondered, or what is become of them? They could not be far
off, and must, at all events, soon join me. In that expectation
I walked my panting Lithuanian to a spring in the market-
place, and let him drink. He drunk uncommonly—with an
eagerness not to be satisfied, but natural enough, for when I
looked round for my men, what should I see? Why, the hind
part of the poor creature, croup and legs were missing, as if
he had been cut in two, and the water ran out as it came in,
without either refreshing him or doing him any good. How
it could have happened was quite a mystery to me, till I
returned with him to the town gate. There I saw that when
I rushed in the flying enemy dropped the portcullis, and
unperceived by me, and the spirited animal, it had totally cut
off his hind part, which lay still quivering on the outside of
the gate. It would have been an irreparable loss, had not our
farrier contrived to bring both parts together while hot. He
sowed them up with sprigs and young shoots of laurels that
were just at hand—the wound healed and what could not
have happened, but to so glorious a horse, the sprigs took
root in his body, grew up, and formed a bower over me, so
that afterwards I could go upon many other expeditions in
the shade of my own and my horse's laurels.

CHAPTER FIVE

In time of war, more than any other, Fortune is a fickle dame. Soon after this I had the misfortune to be overpowered by numbers, to be made prisoner of war; and what is worse, but always usual among the Turks, to be sold for a slave. In that state of humiliation, my daily task was not very hard, and laborious, but rather singular and irksome. It was to drive the Sultan's bees every morning to their pasture grounds, to attend them all the day long and against night to drive them back to their hives. One evening I missed a bee, and soon observed that two bears had fallen upon her, to tear her to pieces for the honey she carried. I had nothing like an offensive weapon in my hands, but the silver hatchet, which is the badge of the Sultan's gardeners and farmers. I threw it at the robbers with an intention to frighten them away, and set the poor bee at liberty; but by an unlucky turn of my arm, it flew upward—and flew, and flew, till it reached the moon. How should I recover it? How fetch it down again? I recollected that Turkey beans grew very quick, and run up to an astonishing height. I planted one immediately, it grew and actually fastened itself to one of the moon's horns. I had no more to do now, but to climb up by it into the moon, where I safely arrived.

I had a troublesome piece of work of it, before I could find my silver hatchet in a place where every thing has the brightness of silver. At last however I found it in a heap of chaff and chopped straw.

I was now for returning, but alas, the heat of the sun had dried up my bean and it was totally useless for my descent. So I fell to work, and twisted me a rope of that chopped straw, as long and well as I could make it. This I fastened to one of the moon's horns, and slid down to the end of it. Here I held myself fast with the left hand, and with the hatchet in my right, I cut the long, now useless end of the upper part, which when tied to the lower end brought me a good deal lower. However, this repeated splicing and tying of the rope did not improve its quality nor bring me down to the Sultan's farms. I was still a couple of miles in the clouds when it broke, and with such violence I fell to the ground that I found myself stunned, and in a hole nine fathoms under grass, when I recovered, hardly knowing how to get out again. There was no other way than to go home for a spade and to dig me out by slopes, which I fortunately accomplished, before I had been so much as missed by the steward.

Whilst I am about it, let me recall an entertaining incident that occurred at the outset of the Russo-Turkish war. A certain general had been given an important command. His corps was encamped in a village near the Turkish frontier, and I and my hussars were quartered hard by.

Early one morning I, being at leisure, met a peasant going into the forest to collect nuts and pine kernels for the commanding officer's wife, who was fond of such delicacies, although personally I do not care for them. I decided to go with the peasant and we soon found quantities of what we sought. Of course, we had to dismount to do our gathering, and when we had sufficient, we carried what we had collected back to the cart and filled the waiting sacks. Then we returned for more.

Soon the cart was half full and we were still occupied some distance from the vehicle when we heard a strange growling. Looking up, we saw a huge bear who had smelled the nuts, which are favourites with bears too. Master Bruin had climbed into the cart and was thoroughly enjoying himself. He had dipped a paw into the nearest sack, and was busy cramming a fistful of nuts into his greedy maw.

The peasant could only gape and scratch behind his ear. 'Damnation!' I cried. 'To think I have left my gun lying in the cart!' The bear was standing close by it, and squinting about him with every sign of contentment, as he coolly helped himself to another pawful of nuts.

The peasant was speechless, but his horse could smell the bear and became very agitated, tossing its head nervously from right to left. Then the man recovered his presence of mind enough to shout to his nag: 'Gee up!' The piebald started up at a trot directly, making for the road. This sadly upset the bear, who did not trust himself to jump down from the moving vehicle, and he began to roar in a most hair-raising fashion.

The noise, of course, only made the nag increase its speed, and once it had reached the smooth high-road, it went tearing along at a great pace, making straight for the camp where the troops were stationed, with the bear standing upright in the cart, roaring its head off.

Now the troops were expecting the general to come and inspect them that very morning, and the whole corps was drawn up on parade. The mayor and civic dignitaries had arrived from the nearest town, and spectators were streaming along in their hundreds. There was a full muster of troops, infantry and cavalry, chasseurs, pioneers, gunners and all.

A great cloud of dust could now be seen whirling along the highway. The pipers placed their instruments to their lips, the ensigns and flag officers stood to attention, and the cloud of dust came nearer and nearer. As soon as the rattle

of wheels was heard, the commanding officer gave a shout: 'Here comes the general!' and then he gave the signal. The band struck up the National Anthem, the drummers beat a tattoo, banners were dipped and a thousand voices thundered: 'Three cheers for his Excellency! Long live the general!' And then: 'Hip, hip, hoorah!'

In the midst of all the tumultuous acclaim along galloped the peasant's piebald, only to collapse in the shafts at the moment of its arrival. There, amid the slumping sacks, stood the frantic bear, who had quite overdone his growling and had now lost his voice. He gazed around him, panic-stricken.

The peasant and I had pursued the triumphal procession down the high-road with all the speed at our command. The peasant, naturally, was soon left behind, and I even I was quite out of breath after such a marathon spurt. I reached the cart the very moment it stopped and as I grasped the brute's short stump of a tail, one thin voice could still be heard shouting for the last time: 'Long live the general!'

I gave the bear's tail a powerful tug, and the recipient of the grand welcome was jerked from the cart and fell to the ground with such force that he broke both neck and ribs. The music stopped, the cheering died away and the commandant broke the ensuing silence. 'But Baron Munchausen,' he exclaimed. 'This is not his Excellency!'

'Your obedient servant, sir,' I replied. 'No indeed. This is not the general. It is a wild bear with a dozen sacks of nuts.'

And that was the end of the bear who impersonated a general. As a punishment for his impertinence he was sentenced to be stuffed, and you will find him in the Natural History Museum in Kiev if you happen to pass that way.

Peace was soon after concluded with the Turks, and I recovered my liberty. When I left St Petersburgh for Europe the winter was then so uncommonly severe that

I saw Hans dipping lower and lower, until he fell into the sea. (See page 49)

ever since the sun seems to be frost-bitten! At my return I
felt on the road greater inconveniences than those I had
experienced in my setting out for Russia. I travelled post
day and night, and finding myself engaged in a narrow lane,
I bid the postillion give a signal with his horn, that other
travellers might not meet or stop us in the narrow passage.
He blew with all his might, but all his endeavours were in
vain. He could not make the horn speak, which, as he pre-
tended to be a good performer, was as unaccountable to him,
as to me, and rather unfortunately, for soon after we found
ourselves in the presence of another coach coming the other
way. It was very troublesome for both parties in this horrid
weather, for there was no proceeding either way, without
taking the carriages to pieces and putting them together
again, past each other. By the time this was completed my
poor postillion and everybody was almost froze to death.
However we reached the much-looked-for stage, without
further accident, and well pleased and happy in our minds,
we all of us hastened to warm and refresh ourselves.

The postillion hung his great coat and horn on a peg and
sat down near the kitchen fire, to forget and drown his cares.
I sat down on the other side doing the same. Suddenly we
heard a *Tereng! tereng, teng, teng!* We looked round, and now
found the reason, why the postillion had not been able to
sound his horn. His tunes were frozen up in the horn, and
came out now by thawing, plain enough, and much to the
credit of the driver, so that the honest fellow entertained us
for some time with a variety of tunes, without putting his
mouth to the horn. The King of Prussia's march—Over the
hill and over the dale—An evening hymn, and many other
favourite tunes came out, and the thawing entertainment
concluded, as I shall this short account of my Russian travels,
with

God bless Great George our King.

CHAPTER SIX

I embarked at Portsmouth in a first-rate English man-o'-war, of one hundred guns, and fourteen hundred men, for North America. Nothing worth relating happened till we arrived within three hundred leagues of the river St Lawrence, when the ship struck with amazing force against (as we supposed) a rock; however, upon heaving the lead we could find no bottom, even with three hundred fathom. What made this circumstance the more wonderful, and indeed beyond all comprehension, was, that the violence of the shock was such that we lost our rudder, broke our bowsprit in the middle, and split all our masts from top to bottom, two of which went by the board. A poor fellow, who was aloft furling the mainsheet, was flung at least three leagues from the ship; but he fortunately saved his life by laying hold of the tail of a large seagull, who brought him back, and lodged him on the very spot from whence he was thrown.

Another proof of the violence of the shock was the force with which the people between decks were driven against the floors above them: my head particularly was pressed into my stomach, where it continued some months before it recovered its natural situation.

Whilst we were all in a state of astonishment at the general and unaccountable confusion in which we were involved, the whole was suddenly explained by the appearance of a large whale, who had been basking, asleep, within sixteen feet of the surface of the water. This animal was so much displeased with the disturbance which our ship had given him (for in our passage we had with our rudder scratched his nose) that he beat in all the gallery and part of the quarter-deck with his tail, and almost at the same instant took the main-sheet anchor, which was suspended, as it usually is, from the head, between his teeth, and ran away with the ship, at least sixty leagues, at the rate of twelve leagues an hour, when fortunately the cable broke, and we lost both the whale and the anchor.

However, upon our return to Europe, some months after, we found the same whale, within a few leagues of the same spot, floating dead upon the water; it measured above half a mile in length. As we could take but a small quantity of such a monstrous animal on board, we got our boats out, and with much difficulty cut off his head, where, to our great joy, we found the anchor, and above forty fathom of the cable, concealed on the left side of his mouth, just under his tongue. This was the only extraordinary circumstance that happened on this voyage.

One part of our distress however I had like to have forgot: while the whale was running away with the ship, she sprung a leak, and the water poured in so fast, that all our pumps could not keep us from sinking; it was however my good fortune to discover it first. I found it a large hole about a foot diameter; and you will be glad to know that this noble vessel was preserved, with all its crew, by a most fortunate thought! In short, I completely filled it with my posterior, without taking off my small-clothes, and indeed I could have done so had the hole been larger still. For I am commonly considered to be somewhat broad in the beam.

My situation, while I sat there, was rather cool, but the carpenter's art soon relieved me.

I was once in great danger of being lost in a most singular manner in the Mediterranean: I was bathing in that pleasant sea near Marseilles one summer's afternoon, when I discovered a very large fish, with his jaws quite extended, approaching me with the greatest velocity; there was no time to be lost, nor could I possibly avoid him. I immediately reduced myself to as small a size as possible, by closing my feet and placing my hands also near my sides, in which position I passed directly between his jaws, and into his stomach, where I remained some time in total darkness, and comfortably warm, as you may imagine.

At last it occurred to me, that by giving him pain he would be glad to get rid of me: as I had plenty of room, I played my pranks, such as tumbling, hop, step, and jump, and so on, but nothing seemed to disturb him so much as the quick motion of my feet in attempting to dance a hornpipe; soon after I began he put me out, by sudden fits and starts: I persevered; at last he was discovered by the people on board an Italian trader, then sailing by, who harpooned him in a few minutes. As soon as he was brought on board, I heard the crew consulting how they should cut him up, so as to preserve the greatest quantity of oil. As I understood Italian, I was in most dreadful apprehensions lest their weapons employed in this business should destroy me also; therefore I stood as near the centre as possible, for there was room enough for a dozen men in this creature's stomach, and I naturally imagined they would begin with the extremities: however, my fears were soon dispersed, for they began by opening the bottom of the belly. As soon as I perceived a glimmering of light I called out lustily to be released from a situation in which I was now almost suffocated. It is impossible for me to do justice to the degree and kind of astonishment which sat upon every countenance at hearing a human voice issue from a fish, but more so at seeing a naked man walk upright out of his body: in short, gentlemen, I told them the whole story, as I have done you, whilst amazement struck them dumb.

After taking some refreshment, and jumping into the sea to cleanse myself, I swam to my clothes, which lay where I had left them on the shore. As near as I can calculate, I was near four hours and a half confined in the stomach of this animal.

CHAPTER SEVEN

When I was in the service of the Turks I frequently amused myself in a pleasure-barge on the Marmora, which commands a view of the whole city of Constantinople, including the Grand Seignior's Seraglio. One morning, as I was admiring the beauty and serenity of the sky, I observed a globular substance in the air, which appeared to be about the size of a twelve-inch globe, with something suspended from it. I immediately took up my largest and longest barrel fowling piece. I charged it with ball, and fired at the globe; but to no purpose, the object being at too great a distance. I then put in a double quantity of powder, and five or six balls: this second attempt succeeded; all the balls took effect, and tore one side open, and brought it down. Judge my surprise, when a most elegant gilt car, with a man in it, and part of a sheep which seemed to have been roasted, fell within two yards of me. When my astonishment had in some degree subsided, I ordered my people to row close to this strange aerial traveller.

I took him on board my barge (he was a native of France) and he was much indisposed from his sudden fall into the sea, and incapable of speaking. After some time, however, he recovered and gave the following account of himself: 'About seven or eight days since, I cannot tell which, for I have lost my reckoning, having been most of the time where the sun never sets, I ascended from the Land's-End in Cornwall, in the island of Great Britain, in the car from which I have been just taken, suspended from a very large balloon, and took a sheep with me, to try atmospheric experiments upon. Unfortunately, the wind changed within ten minutes after my ascent; and, instead of driving towards Exeter, where I intended to land, I was driven towards the sea, over which I suppose I have continued ever since, but much too high to make observations.

'The calls of hunger were so pressing, that the intended experiments upon heat and respiration gave way to them. I was obliged, on the third day, to kill the sheep for food; and being at that time infinitely above the moon, and for upwards of sixteen hours after so very near the sun that it scorched my eyebrows, I placed the carcase, taking care to skin it first, in that part of the car where the sun had sufficient power, or, in other words, where the balloon did not shade it from the sun, by which method it was well roasted in about two hours. This has been my food ever since.' Here he paused, and seemed lost in viewing the objects about him. When I told him the buildings before us were the Grand Seignior's Seraglio at Constantinople, he seemed exceedingly affected, as he had supposed himself in a very different situation. 'The cause,' added he, 'of my long flight, was owing to the failure of a string which was fixed to a valve in the balloon, intended to let out the inflammable air; and if it had not been fired at, and rent in the manner before mentioned, I might, like Mahomet, have been suspended between heaven and earth till doomsday.'

CHAPTER EIGHT

The Grand Seignior employed me to negotiate a matter of great importance at Grand Cairo. I went there in great state by land and having completed the business successfully I dismissed almost all my attendants, and returned like a private gentleman. The weather was delightful, and that famous river the Nile was beautiful beyond all description; in short, I was tempted to hire a barge to descend by water to Alexandria. On the third day of my voyage the river began to rise most amazingly (you have heard, I presume, of the annual overflowing of the Nile), and on the next day it spread over the whole country for many leagues on each side.

On the fifth, at sunrise, my barge became entangled with what I at first took for shrubs; but as the light became stronger I found myself surrounded by almonds, which were perfectly ripe, and in the highest perfection. Upon plumbing with a line my people found we were at least sixty feet from the ground, and unable to advance or retreat. At about eight or nine o'clock, as near as I could judge by the altitude of the sun, the wind rose suddenly, and canted our barge on one side: here she filled, and I saw no more of her for some time. Fortunately we all saved ourselves (six men and two boys) by clinging to the tree, the boughs of which were equal to our weight, though not to that of the barge: in this situation we continued six weeks and three days, living upon the almonds; I need not inform you we had plenty of water.

On the forty-second day of our distress the water fell as rapidly as it had risen, and on the forty-sixth we were able to venture down upon terra firma. Our barge was the first pleasing object we saw, about two hundred yards from the spot where she sunk. After drying everything that was useful by the heat of the sun, and loading ourselves with necessities from the stores on board, we set out to recover our lost ground; and found, by the nearest calculation, we had been carried over garden-walls, and a variety of enclosures, above one hundred and fifty miles. In four days, after a very tiresome journey on foot, we reached the river, which was now confined to its banks, related our adventures to a Bey, who kindly accommodated all our wants, and sent us forward in a barge of his own. In six days more we arrived at Alexandria, where we took shipping for Constantinople. I was received kindly by the Grand Seignior, and had the honour of seeing the Seraglio, to which his highness introduced me himself. That night, we boarded a vessel bound for Venice and thence, made our way home.

CHAPTER NINE

During the late siege of Gibraltar I went with a provision-fleet, under Lord Rodney's command, to see my old friend General Elliot, who has, by his distinguished defence of that place, acquired laurels that can never fade. After the usual joy which generally attends the meeting of old friends had subsided, I went to examine the state of the garrison, and view the operations of the enemy, for which purpose the General accompanied me. I had brought a most excellent refracting telescope with me from London, purchased of the famous firm of Dollond, by the help of which I found the enemy were going to discharge a thirty-six pounder at the spot where we stood. I told the General what they were about; he looked through the glass also, and found my conjectures right. I immediately, by his permission, ordered a forty-eight pounder to be brought from a neighbouring battery, which I placed with so much exactness that I was sure of my mark.

I continued watching the enemy till I saw the match placed at the touch-hole of their piece. At that very instant I gave the signal for our gun to be fired also. About midway between the two pieces of cannon the balls struck each other with amazing force, and the effect was astonishing! The enemy's ball recoiled back with such violence as to kill the man who had discharged it, by carrying his head fairly off, with sixteen others which it met with in its progress to the Barbary Coast; where its force, after passing through three masts of vessels that then lay in a line behind each other in the harbour, was so much spent, that it only broke its way through the roof of a poor labourer's hut, about two hundred yards inland, and destroyed a few teeth an old woman had left, who lay asleep upon her back with her mouth open. The ball lodged in her throat. Her husband soon after came home, and endeavoured to extract it; but finding that impracticable, by the assistance of a rammer he forced it into her stomach from whence it was discharged downwards in a natural way.

Our ball did excellent service; for it not only repelled the other in the manner just described; but proceeding as I intended it should, it dismounted the very piece of cannon that had been just employed against us, and forced it into the hold of the ship, where it fell with so much force as to break its way through the bottom. The ship immediately filled and sunk, with above a thousand Spanish sailors on board, besides a considerable number of soldiers. This, to be sure, was a most extraordinary exploit: I will not, however, take the whole merit to myself. Chance assisted me a little; for I afterwards found, that the man who charged our forty-eight pounder put in, by mistake, a double quantity of powder, else we could never have succeeded so much beyond all expectation, especially in repelling the enemy's ball.

General Elliot would have given me a commission for this singular piece of service; but I declined everything, except his thanks, which I received at a crowded table of officers at supper on the evening of that very day.

As I am very partial to the English, who are beyond all doubt a brave people, I determined not to take my leave of the garrison till I had rendered them another piece of service, and in about three weeks an opportunity presented itself. I dressed myself in the habit of a priest, and at about one

o'clock in the morning stole out of the garrison, passed the
enemy's lines, and arrived in the middle of their camp, where
I entered the tent in which the Count d'Artois was, with the
commander-in-chief, and several other officers, in deep
council, concerning a plan to storm the garrison next
morning. My disguise was my protection; they suffered me
to continue there, hearing everything that passed, till they
went to their several beds. When the whole camp and even
the sentinels, were wrapped up in the arms of Morpheus, I
began my work, which was that of dismounting all their
cannon (above three hundred pieces) from forty-eight to
twenty-four pounders, and throwing them three leagues into
the sea. Having no assistance, I found this the hardest task I
ever undertook. I then piled all the carriages together in the
centre of the camp, which, to prevent the noise of the wheels
being heard, I carried in pairs under my arms: and a noble
appearance they made, as high at least as the rock of
Gibraltar. I then lighted a match by striking a flint stone,
situated twenty feet from the ground with the breech of an
iron eight-and-forty pounder, and so set fire to the whole
pile. I forgot to inform you that I threw all their ammunition-
wagons upon the top.

Before I applied the lighted match I had laid the com-
bustibles at the bottom so judiciously, that the whole was in
a blaze in a moment. To prevent suspicion, I was one of the
first to express my surprise. The whole camp was, as you
may imagine, petrified with astonishment; the general conclusion was, that their sentinels had been bribed, and that
seven or eight regiments of the garrison had been employed
in this horrid destruction of their artillery. Thus I alone
saved Gibraltar by this night's business. The Count d'Artois
and all his attendants ran away in their fright, and never
stopped on the road till they reached Paris.

*If any gentleman will say he doubts the truth of this story, I will
fine him a gallon of brandy and make him drink it at one draught.*

CHAPTER TEN

About two months after I had done the besieged this service, one morning, as I sat at breakfast with General Elliot, a shell (for I had not time to destroy their mortars as well as their cannon) entered the apartment we were sitting in; it lodged upon our table. The General, as most men would do, quitted the room directly; but I took it up before it burst, and carried it to the top of the rock; when, looking over the enemy's camp, on an eminence near the sea-coast, I observed a considerable number of people, but could not, with my naked eye, discover how they were employed. I had recourse again to my telescope, when I found that two of our officers, one a general, the other a colonel, with whom I had spent the preceding evening, and who went out into the enemy's camp about midnight as spies, were taken, and then were actually going to be executed on a gibbet. I found the distance too great to throw the shell with my hand, but most fortunately recollecting that I had the very sling in my pocket which assisted David in slaying Goliath, I placed the shell in it, and immediately threw it in the midst of them: it burst as it fell, and destroyed all present, except the two culprits, who were saved by being suspended so high, for they were just turned off: however, one of the pieces of the shell fled with such force against the foot of the gibbet, that it immediately brought it down.

Our two friends no sooner felt terra firma, than they looked about for the cause; and finding their guards, executioner, and all, had taken it in their heads to die first, they directly extricated each other from their disgraceful cords and then ran down to the seashore, seized a Spanish boat with two men in it, and made them row to one of our ships, which they did with great safety; and in a few minutes after, when I was relating to General Elliot how I had acted, they both took us by the hand, and, after mutual congratulations, we retired to spend the day with festivity. As to the sling, I have bequeathed it as a relic of inestimable value, to be hung up in Liberty Hall, and hereafter used, as often as necessary, in the destruction of all Tyrants and those who are base enough to act under them.

I do not doubt that you wonder how I became possessed of such a treasure as the sling just mentioned. It is quite simple. I am a direct descendant of that King David whom we read of in the Bible and the sling has, without interruption, descended from father to son to this very day.

One of its possessors, my great great grandfather, who lived about two hundred and fifty years ago, was upon a visit to England, and became intimate with a poet, who was a great deer-stealer; I think his name was Shakespeare: he frequently borrowed this sling, and with it killed so much of Sir Thomas Lucy's venison, that he narrowly escaped the fate of my two friends at Gibraltar.

My father, who was the immediate possessor of this sling before me, told me the following anecdote:

He was walking by the sea-shore at Harwich, with this sling in his pocket; before his paces had covered a mile he was attacked by a fierce animal called a seahorse, openmouthed, who ran at him with great fury; he hesitated a moment, then took out his sling, retreated back about a hundred yards, stooped for a couple of pebbles, of which there were plenty under his feet, and slung them both so dexterously at the animal, that each stone put out an eye, and lodged in the cavities which their removal had occasioned. He now got upon its back, and drove him into the sea; for the moment he lost his sight he lost also his ferocity, and became as tame as possible: the sling was placed as a bridle in his mouth; he was guided with the greatest facility across the ocean, and in less than three hours they both arrived on the opposite shore, which is about thirty leagues. The master of the *Three Cups*, at Helvoetsluys, in Holland, purchased this marine horse, to make an exhibition of, for seven hundred ducats, which was upwards of three hundred pounds, and the next day my father paid his passage back in the packet to Harwich.

This famous sling makes the possessor equal to any task he is desirous of performing, and with it I made a balloon of such extensive dimensions, that an account of the silk it contained would exceed all credibility; every mercer's shop and weaver's stock in London, Westminster, and Spitalfields contributed to it. With this balloon and my sling I played many tricks, such as taking one house from its station, and placing another in its stead, without disturbing the inhabitants, who were generally asleep, or too much employed to observe the peregrinations of their habitations. When the sentinel at Windsor Castle heard St Paul's clock strike thirteen, it was through my dexterity; I brought the buildings close together that night, by placing the castle in St George's Fields, and carried it back again before daylight, without waking any of the inhabitants. Notwithstanding these exploits, I should have kept my balloon and its properties a secret, if Montgolfier had not made the art of flying so public.

On the 30th of September, when the College of Physicians

I was shot over the houses ... (See page 55)

chose their annual officers, and dined sumptuously together, I filled my balloon, brought it over the dome of their building, clapped the sling round the golden ball at the top, fastening the other end of it to the balloon and immediately ascended with the whole college to an immense height, where I kept them upwards of three months. You will naturally inquire what they did for food such a length of time? To this I answer: Had I kept them suspended twice the time, they would have experienced no inconvenience on that account, so amply, or rather extravagantly, had they spread their table for that day's feasting.

Though this was meant as an innocent frolic, it was productive of much mischief to several respectable characters amongst the clergy, undertakers, sextons, and gravediggers: they were, it must be acknowledged, sufferers; for it is a well-known fact, that during the three months the college was suspended in the air, and therefore incapable of attending their patients, no deaths happened, except a few who fell before the scythe of Father Time.

Indeed, if the apothecaries had not been very active during the above time, half the undertakers in all probability would have been bankrupts.

On my return from Gibraltar I travelled by way of France to England. Being a foreigner, this was not attended with any inconvenience to me in spite of the hostility between those two countries when the American colonies were asserting their independence. I found, in the harbour of Calais, a ship just arrived with a number of English sailors as prisoners of war. I immediately conceived an idea of giving these brave fellows their liberty, which I accomplished as follows: After forming a pair of large wings, each of them forty yards long, and fourteen wide, and annexing them to myself, I mounted at break of day, when every creature, even the watch upon deck, was fast asleep. As I hovered over the ship I fastened three grappling irons to the tops of the three masts with my sling, and fairly lifted her several yards out of the water, and then proceeded across to Dover, where I arrived in half an hour!

As to the prisoners, and the Frenchmen who guarded them, they did not awake till they had been near two hours on Dover Pier. The moment the English understood their situation they changed places with their guard, and took back what they had been plundered of, but no more, for they were too generous to retaliate and plunder them in return.

With Captain Phipps I also paid a visit to a high northern latitude where I was viewing the objects around me with the telescope, which I introduced to your notice in my Gibraltar adventures. I thought I saw two large white bears in violent action upon a body of ice considerably above the masts, and about half a league distance. I immediately took my carbine, slung it across my shoulder, and ascended the ice. When I arrived at the top, the unevenness of the surface made my approach to those animals troublesome and hazardous beyond expression. Sometimes hideous cavities opposed me, which I was obliged to spring over; in other parts the surface was as smooth as a mirror, and I was continually falling.

As I approached near enough to reach them, I found they were only at play. Judge of my surprise when one of those large animals I have been just describing had turned me upon my face, and was laying hold of the waistband of my breeches. He was certainly going to carry me feet foremost, God knows where, when I took a large clasp knife out of my side pocket, made a chop at one of his hind-feet, and cut off three of his toes. He immediately let me drop and roared most horridly. I took up my carbine and fired at him as he ran off; he fell directly.

The noise of the piece roused several thousands of these white bears, who were asleep upon the ice within half a mile of me; they came immediately to the spot. There was no time to be lost. I took off the skin and head of the dead bear in half the time that some people would be in skinning a rabbit, and wrapped myself in it, placing my own head directly under Bruin's; the whole herd came round me immediately, and my apprehensions threw me into a most piteous situation to be sure: however, my scheme turned out a most admirable one for my own safety. They all came smelling, and evidently took me for a brother Bruin. After they had all smelt me, and the body of their deceased companion, whose skin was now become my protector, we seemed very sociable, and I found I could mimic all their actions tolerably well; but at growling, roaring, and hugging they were quite my masters. I began now to think how I might turn the general confidence which I had created amongst these animals to my advantage.

I had heard an old army surgeon say a wound in the spine was instant death. I now determined to try the experiment, and had again recourse to my knife, with which I struck the largest in the back of the neck. I was remarkably fortunate, for he fell dead at my feet without making the least noise. I was now resolved to demolish them every one in the same manner, which I accomplished without the least difficulty; for although they saw their companions fall, they had no suspicion of either the cause or the effect. When they all lay dead before me, I felt myself a second Sampson, having slain my thousands.

To make short of the story, I went back to the ship, and borrowed three parts of the crew to assist me in skinning them, and carrying the hams on board, which we did in a few hours, and loaded the ship with them.

As soon as we returned I sent some of the hams, in the captain's name, to the Lords of the Admiralty, others to the Lords of the Treasury, some to the Lord Mayor and Corporation of London, a few to each of the trading companies, and the remainder to my particular friends, from all of whom I received warm thanks; but from the city I was honoured with substantial notice, viz., an invitation to dine at Guildhall annually on Lord Mayor's day.

The bear-skins I sent to Catherine, Empress of Russia, to clothe her majesty and her court in the winter, for which she wrote me a letter of thanks with her own hand.

CHAPTER ELEVEN

I omitted several very material parts in my father's journey across the English Channel to Holland, which, that they may not be totally lost, I will now faithfully give you in his own words, as I heard him relate them to his friends several times.

'On my arrival,' says my father, 'at Helvoetsluys, I was observed to breathe with some difficulty: upon the inhabitants inquiring into the cause, I informed them that the animal upon whose back I rode from Harwich across to their shore did not swim! Such is their peculiar form and disposition, that they cannot float or move upon the surface of the water; he ran with incredible swiftness upon the sands from shore to shore, driving fish in millions before him, many of which were quite different, from any I had yet seen, carrying their heads at the extremity of their tails.

'I crossed,' continued he, 'one prodigious range of rocks, equal in height to the Alps (the tops or highest, part of these marine mountains are said to be upwards of one hundred fathoms below the surface of the sea), on the sides of which there was a great variety of tall, noble trees, loaded with marine fruit, such as lobsters, crabs, oysters, scollops, mussels, cockles, and many others; some of which were a

cart-load singly! and none less than a porter's! All those
which are brought on shore and sold in our markets are of
an inferior dwarf kind, or, properly, waterfalls, i.e. fruit
shook off the branches of the tree it grows upon by the
motion of the water, as those in our gardens are by that of the
wind! The lobster-trees appeared the richest, but the crab and
oysters were the tallest. The periwinkle is a kind of shrub; it
grows at the foot of the oyster-tree, and twines round it, as
the ivy does the oak.

'I observed the effect of several accidents by shipwreck,
particularly a ship that had been wrecked by striking against
a mountain or rock, the top of which lay within three
fathoms of the surface. As she sunk she fell upon her side,
and forced a very large lobster-tree out of its place. It was in
the spring, when the lobsters were very young, and many of
them being separated by the violence of the shock, they fell
upon a crab-tree which was growing below them; they have,
like the farina of plants, united, and produced a fish resemb-
ling both. I endeavoured to bring one with me, but it was too
cumbersome, and my salt-water Pegasus seemed much displeased at every attempt to stop his career whilst I continued
upon his back; besides, I then began to find the want of air
inconvenient; therefore I had no inclination to prolong the
time. Add to this, my situation was in other respects very
unpleasant; I met many large fish, who were, if I could judge
by their open mouths, not only able, but really wished to
devour us; now, as my Rosinante was blind, I had these
hungry gentlemen's attempts to guard against, in addition
to my other difficulties.

'As we drew near the Dutch shore, and the body of water
over our heads did not exceed twenty fathoms, I thought I
saw a human figure in a female dress then lying on the sand
before me, with some signs of life; when I came close I perceived her hand move: I took it into mine, and brought her
on shore as a corpse. An apothecary, who had just been

instructed by Dr Hawes of London in his particular skill known as artificial respiration, treated her properly, and she recovered. She was the rib of a man who commanded a vessel belonging to Helvoetsluys, and even he had given her up for dead.'

CHAPTER TWELVE

Some years ago when I was neither man nor boy, but between both, I expressed in repeated conversations a strong desire of seeing the world, from which I was discouraged by my parents. A cousin, by my mother's side, took a liking to me, often said I was a fine forward youth, and was much inclined to gratify my curiosity. His eloquence had more effect than mine, for my father consented to my accompanying him in a voyage to the island of Ceylon, where his uncle had resided as governor many years.

We sailed from Amsterdam and the only circumstance which happened on our voyage worth relating, was the wonderful effects of a storm, which had torn up by the roots a great number of trees of enormous bulk and height, in an island where we lay at anchor to take in wood and water; some of these trees weighed many tons, yet they were carried by the wind so amazingly high, that they appeared like the feathers of small birds floating in the air, for they were at least five miles above the earth. However, as soon as the storm subsided, they all fell perpendicularly into their respective places, and took root again, except the largest, which happened, when it was blown into the air, to have a man and his wife, a very honest old couple, upon its branches, gathering cucumbers (in this part of the globe, that useful vegetable grows upon trees). The weight of this couple, as the tree descended, over-balanced the trunk, and brought it down in a horizontal position. The tree fell upon the chief man of the island, and killed him on the spot; he had quitted his house in the storm, under an apprehension of its falling upon him, and was returning through his own garden when this fortunate accident happened. The word fortunate, here, requires some explanation. This chief was a man of a very avaricious and oppressive disposition, and the natives of the island were half starved by his tyrannical and infamous impositions.

The very goods which he had thus taken from them were spoiling in his stores, while the poor wretches from whom they were plundered were pining in poverty. Though the destruction of this tyrant was accidental, the people chose the cucumber-gatherers for their governors, as a mark of their gratitude for destroying, though accidentally, their late tyrant.

After we had repaired the damages we sustained in this re-markable storm, and taken leave of the new governor and his lady, we sailed with a fair wind for the object of our voyage.

In about six weeks we arrived at Ceylong, and after we had resided there about a fortnight, I accompanied one of the governor's brothers upon a shooting party. He was a strong, athletic man, and being used to that climate he bore the violent heat of the sun much better than I could; in our excursion he had made a considerable progress through a thick wood when I was only at the entrance.

Near the banks of a large piece of water, which had en-gaged my attention, I thought I heard a rustling noise behind; on turning about I was almost petrified (as who would not?) at the sight of a lion, which was evidently approaching with the intention of satisfying his appetite with my poor carcase, and that without asking my consent. What was to be done in this horrible dilemma? I had not

I found a large crocodile, with his mouth extended almost ready to receive me

even a moment for reflection; my piece was only charged with swan-shot, and I had no other about me. However, though I could have no idea of killing such an animal with that weak kind of ammunition, yet I had some hopes of frightening him by the report, and perhaps of wounding him also. I immediately let fly, without waiting till he was within reach; and the report did but enrage him, for he now quickened his pace, and seemed to approach me full speed.

I attempted to escape, but that only added (if an addition could be made) to my distress; for the moment I turned about, I found a large crocodile, with his mouth extended almost ready to receive me; on my right hand was the piece of water before mentioned, and on my left a deep precipice, said to have, as I have since learned, a receptacle at the bottom for venomous creatures. In short, I gave myself up as lost, for the lion was now upon his hind-legs, just in the act of seizing me.

I fell involuntarily to the ground with fear, and, as it afterwards appeared, he sprang over me. I lay some time in a situation which no language can describe, expecting to feel his teeth or talons in some part of me every moment. After waiting in this prostrate situation a few seconds, I heard a violent but unusual noise, different from any sound that had ever before assailed my ears; nor is it at all to be wondered at, when I inform you from whence it proceeded: after listening for some time, I ventured to raise my head and look round. To my unspeakable joy, I perceived the lion had, by the eagerness with which he sprung at me, jumped forward, as I fell, into the crocodile's mouth which, as before observed, was wide open. The head of the one stuck in the throat of the other and they were struggling to extricate themselves. I fortunately recollected my hunting knife which was by my side. With this instrument I severed the lion's head at one blow, and the body fell at my feet! I then, with the butt end of my fowling-piece, rammed the head farther into the throat of the crocodile, and destroyed him by suffocation, for he could neither gorge nor eject it.

Soon after I had thus gained a complete victory over my two powerful adversaries, my companion arrived in search of me; for, finding I did not follow him into the wood, he returned, apprehending I had lost my way, or met with some accident.

After mutual congratulations, we measured the crocodile, which was just forty feet in length.

As soon as we had related this extraordinary adventure to the governor, he sent a waggon and servants, who brought home the two carcases. The lion's skin was properly preserved, with its hair on; after which it was made into tobacco-pouches, and presented by me upon our return to Holland to the burgomasters, who in return, requested my acceptance of a thousand ducats. The skin of the crocodile was stuffed in the usual manner, and makes a capital article in their public museum at Amsterdam.

In a voyage which I made to the East Indies with Captain Hamilton, I took a favourite pointer with me; he was, to use a common phrase, worth his weight in gold, for he never deceived me. One day when we were, by the best observations we could make, at least three hundred leagues from land, my dog pointed. I observed him for near an hour with astonishment, and mentioned the circumstance to the captain and every officer on board, asserting that we must be near land, for my dog smelt game. This occasioned a general laugh, but that did not alter in the least the good opinion I had of my dog. After much conversation pro and con, I boldly told the captain I placed more confidence in Tray's nose than I did in the eyes of every seaman on board, and therefore proposed laying the sum I had agreed to pay for my passage (viz., one hundred guineas), that we should find game within half an hour.

Done! and Done! were scarcely said on both sides, when

some sailors who were fishing in the long-boat, which was made fast to the stern of the ship, harpooned an exceeding large shark, which they brought on board, and began to cut up for the purpose of barrelling the oil, when, behold, they found no less than *six brace of live partridges* in this animal's stomach!

They had been so long in that situation, that one of the hens was sitting upon four eggs, and a fifth was hatching when the shark was opened! This young bird we brought up by placing it with a litter of kittens that came into the world a few minutes before! The old cat was as fond of it as of any of her own four-legged progeny, and made herself very unhappy when it flew out of her reach till it returned again. As to the other partridges, there were four hens amongst them: one or more were, during the voyage, constantly sitting, and consequently we had plenty of game at the captain's table; and in gratitude to poor Tray (for being a means of winning one hundred guineas), I ordered him the bones daily, and sometimes a whole bird.

CHAPTER THIRTEEN

This voyage ended in disaster, however, for our ship sank in a gale. I was the sole survivor and forced to rely on my prowess at swimming in order to save my life. But in which direction ought I to go? There was nothing to guide me, nothing but sky and water around me, and it was becoming uncomfortably cool, not to say cold. Anyone else in my situation would have given up in despair, but I calmly took stock of my predicament. At last, I espied in the distance a dug-out canoe containing five savages and one white man, who were engaged in hunting sea-cows. I hullooed as loudly as I could to attract their attention and then I swam rapidly towards them, presently reaching the canoe. The men helped me on board and the white man told me that he was a Dutchman, Hans by name, the only survivor of a vessel wrecked against the reef of a hitherto uncharted island in the Southern Ocean.

On the way to this island, the Dutchman told me that the ruler was a good-hearted prince, but unfortunately he was most partial to roast human flesh, preferably that of a foreigner. It tastes best, so it seems, after the victim has been fattened on a strictly vegetarian diet of nuts and other tropical fruits. Hans had himself been fattened in this manner, but shortly before he was considered ready, there had been a storm and it had rained meat pasties, which he had eaten with great relish. At this, the prince grew very angry, declaring that the delicate flavour would be quite spoilt, so he had ordered another month's fattening, after which the Dutchman would be roasted immediately and eaten.

In the course of our conversation, we had come close to the island, and the prince was already seated on the shore, awaiting our arrival. The Dutchman introduced me with all my titles, at which the prince nodded graciously and whispered to his Prime Minister: 'Have him fattened at once!' A truly pleasant prospect for me!

Thus I found little pleasure in my sojourn in the Southern Seas, for even the prospect of a rich diet of tropical fruits, if it were to be followed by being served as a dainty morsel for the prince's table, made no appeal to me. Therefore I looked for an occasion for a private conversation with my friend the Dutchman, and I found it that very evening. I informed him that it was my intention to arrange our escape from the island together at the first opportunity, at which he was delighted. We discussed the possibility of building a boat in secret and fitting it out. I asked what kind of timber grew in those parts, and if the trees here were not a species of tulip tree, as I believed from the shape of their fruits.

'That I do not know,' answered Hans, 'but as I observe, the fruits are like gourds or hollow bladders, in appearance like small balloons. The natives always pluck these fruits before they ripen completely, for otherwise the heat of the sun would so expand the air inside them, that the numerous balloons would raise the tree into the air and uproot it altogether. In fact, the wind would be able to lift it high and carry it away out of sight.'

At this, an idea struck me and embracing Hans, I cried joyfully: 'Why, man, this is the answer! Tell me, when will the trees be stripped?'

'Hm. Probably some time during the next few days.'

'Really! And what do they do with the fruits?'

'Oh, they tie them together in dozens, and leave them lying in the sun. In this way, they swell and become light and then they fly up into the air, off and away. When this happens, the day is celebrated with feasting and it is called the Carnival of the Flying Gourds.'

That was enough for me. I made further investigations and a few small experiments. Hans agreed to obtain provisions, which we shared and stowed away in our pockets. When, on one of the following days, the little balloons all tied together in dozens, were left on the ground in the sunshine, I furtively attached eight or ten of these bunches to my belt and Hans did the same. Soon the air in them grew warm and expanded to such a degree that almost at one and the same moment we were lifted into the air by these bladders, and floated far out to sea on the blustery west wind that had just sprung up.

We were parted from one another almost immediately, but from an ever increasing distance, I saw Hans dipping lower and lower, until he fell into the sea. However, he was soon fished out by a passing schooner, and as I learned later, he got home safe and sound. He is at present employed as curator at the Natural History Museum in Amsterdam, or perhaps it is Leyden, and anyone can go there and question him, where he will readily confirm all I have related here.

I myself was seized by one of those whirlwinds that prevail in the Southern Ocean and which are known in various lands by such names as cyclone, typhoon or hurricane. I was kept whirling hither and thither in the air for three days and three nights, until at last I was overcome by vertigo and fell unconscious into the sea. However, in the cold water I soon recovered my senses, and my extraordinary powers as a swimmer enabled me to catch up with a ship I had seen from a distance of seventeen nautical miles.

Everyone behaved as his foolish head bade him. (See page 83)

On board this Turkish frigate, I was quickly restored to health by a glass of grog so stiff that it could not be drunk at all, but had to be cut up with a knife and eaten with a spoon. The frigate was bound for its home port, so within a few weeks I found myself back in Constantinople, where again I was most kindly received by his Excellency, the Grand Seignior.

CHAPTER FOURTEEN

I have already informed you of one trip I made to the moon, in search of my silver hatchet: I afterwards made another in a much pleasanter manner, and stayed in it long enough to take notice of several things, which I will endeavour to describe as accurately as my memory will permit.

On the eighteenth day after we had passed the Island of Tahiti, mentioned by Captain Cook, a hurricane blew our ship at least one thousand leagues above the surface of the water, and kept it at that height till a fresh gale arising, filled the sails in every part, and onwards we travelled at a prodigious rate; thus we proceeded above the clouds for six weeks. At last we discovered a great land in the sky, like a shining island, round and bright, where coming into a convenient harbour, we went on shore, and soon found it was inhabited. Below us we saw another earth, containing cities, trees, mountains, rivers and seas, which we conjectured was this world which we had left. Here we saw huge figures riding upon vultures of a prodigious size, and each of them having three heads. To form some idea of the magnitude of these birds, I must inform you, that each of their wings is as wide, and six times the length of the main sheet of our vessel, which was about six hundred tons burthen. Thus, instead of riding upon horses, as we do in this world, the inhabitants of the Moon (for we now found we were in madam Luna) fly about on these birds. The king, we found, was engaged in a war with the sun, and he offered me a commission, but I declined the honour his majesty intended me.

Everything in *this* world is of extraordinary magnitude; a common flea being much larger than one of our sheep: in making war, their principal weapons are radishes, which are used as darts; those who are wounded by them, die immediately. Their shields are made of mushrooms, and their darts (when radishes are out of season) of the tops of asparagus. Some of the natives of the dog-star are to be seen here; commerce tempts them to ramble: their faces are like large mastiffs, with their eyes near the lower end or tip of their noses; they have no eyelids, but cover their eyes with the end of their tongues when they go to sleep: they are generally twenty feet high. As to the natives of the Moon, none of them are less in stature than thirty-six feet; they are not called the human species, but 'the cooking animals', for they all dress their food by fire, as we do, but lose no time at their meals, as they open their left side, and place the whole quantity at once in their stomach, then shut it again till the same day in the next month; for they never indulge themselves with food more than twelve times in a year, or once a month. All but gluttons and epicures must prefer this method to ours.

There is but one sex either of the cooking or any other animals in the Moon; they are all produced from trees of various sizes and foliage: that which produces the cooking animal, or human species, is much more beautiful than any of the others; it has large straight boughs, and flesh-coloured leaves, and the fruit it produces are nuts or pods, with hard shells, at least two yards long: when they become ripe, which is known from their changing colour, they are gathered with great care, and laid by as long as they think proper: when they choose to animate the seed of these nuts, they throw them into a large cauldron of boiling water, which opens the shells in a few hours, and out jumps the creature.

Nature forms their minds for different pursuits before they come into the world; from one shell comes forth a warrior, from another a philosopher, from a third a divine, from a fourth a lawyer, from a fifth a farmer, from a sixth a clown, and so it goes. Each of them immediately begins to perfect themselves, by practising what they before knew only in theory.

When they grow old they do not die, but turn into air, and dissolve like smoke! As for their drink, they need none; the only evacuations they have are insensible, and by their breath. They have but one finger upon each hand, with which they perform everything in as perfect a manner as we who have four besides the thumb. Their heads are placed under their right arm; and, when they are going to travel, or about any violent exercise, they generally leave them at home, for they can consult them at any distance; this is a very common practice: and when those of rank or quality among the Lunarians have an inclination to see what's going forward among the common people, they stay at home, i.e. the body stays at home, and sends the head only, which is suffered to be present incognito and return at pleasure with an account of what has passed.

The stones of their grapes are exactly like hail; and I am perfectly satisfied that when a storm or high wind in the Moon shakes their vines, and breaks the grapes from the stalks, the stones fall down and form our hail showers. I would advise those who are of my opinion, to save a quantity of these stones when it hails next, and make Lunarian wine. Some material circumstances I had nearly omitted. They put their bellies to the same use as we do a sack, and throw whatever they have occasion for into it, for they can shut and open it again when they please, as they do their stomachs: they are not troubled with bowels, liver, heart, or any other intestines, neither are they encumbered with clothes, nor is there any part of their bodies unseemly or indecent to exhibit.

Their eyes they can take in and out of their places when they please, and can see as well with them in their hand as in their head! and if by any accident they lose or damage one, they can borrow or purchase another, and see as clearly with it as their own. Dealers in eyes are on that account very numerous in most parts of the Moon, and in this article alone all the inhabitants are whimsical: sometimes green and sometimes yellow eyes are the fashion. I know these things appear strange; but if the shadow of a doubt can remain on any person's mind, I say, let him take a voyage there himself, and then he will know I am a traveller of veracity.

CHAPTER FIFTEEN

My first visit to England was about the beginning of the reign of good King George III. I had occasion to go down to Wapping, to see some goods shipped, which I was sending to some friends at Hamburg: after that business was over, I took the Tower Wharf in my way back. Here I found the sun very powerful; and I was so much fatigued that I stepped into one of the cannon to compose me, where I fell fast asleep. This was about noon; it was the fourth of June, the king's birthday, and exactly at one o'clock these cannon were all discharged in memory of the day. They had been all charged that morning, and having no suspicion of my situation, I was shot over the houses on the opposite side of the river, into a farmer's yard, between Bermondsey and Deptford, where I fell upon a large haystack, without waking, and continued there in a sound sleep till hay became so extravagantly dear (which was about three months after), that the farmer found it his interest to send his whole stock to market: the stack I was reposing upon was the largest in the yard, containing about five hundred load; they began to cut that first. I waked (with the voices of the people who had ascended the ladders to begin at the top), and got up, totally ignorant of my situation; in attempting to run away I fell upon the farmer to whom the hay belonged, and broke his neck, yet received no injury myself! I afterwards found, to my great consolation, that this fellow was a most detestable character, always keeping the produce of his grounds for extravagant markets.

In speaking of His Majesty, I must mention no less a person than his chief coachman, who is a most impressive figure. He wears a wig so long and full that it brushes his shoulders, and his whole chest, right down to his belt is covered by a huge beard, in which the royal coat-of-arms has been most skilfully carved.

When the king drives through the streets of Westminster for the State Opening of Parliament, all eyes are glued on this coachman, and the procession can hardly get by for the admiring crowds. For every time he cracks his whip, the lash forms in mid air the King's royal cipher, that is, the initials G.R. which stands for his name in Latin *Georgius Rex.*

Next, I was induced to pay a visit to Mount Etna in the island of Sicily. One morning early, three or four days after my arrival, I set out from a cottage where I had slept, within six miles of the foot of the mountain, determined to explore the internal parts, if I perished in the attempt. After three hours hard labour I found myself at the top; it was then, and had been for upwards of three weeks, raging. I walked round the edge of the crater, which appeared to be fifty times at least as capacious as the Devil's Punch-Bowl near Petersfield, on the Portsmouth Road, but not so broad at the bottom, as in that part it resembles the contracted part of a funnel more than a punch-bowl. In I sprang feet foremost: I soon found myself in a warm berth, and my body bruised and burnt in various parts by the red-hot cinders, which, by their violent ascent, opposed my descent; however, my weight soon brought me to the bottom, where I found myself in the midst of noise and clamour, mixed with the most horrid imprecations.

I began to look about me. Guess my astonishment, when I found myself in the company of Vulcan and his cyclops, who had been quarrelling, for the three weeks before mentioned, about the observation of good order and due subordination, and which had occasioned such alarms for that space of time in the world above. However, my arrival restored peace to the whole society, and Vulcan himself did me the honour of applying plasters to my wounds, which healed them immediately; he also placed refreshments before me, particularly nectar, and other rich wines, such as the gods and goddesses only aspire to.

After this repast was over Vulcan ordered Venus to show me every indulgence which my situation required. To describe the apartment and the couch on which I reposed, is totally impossible. Let it suffice to say, it exceeds the power of language to do it justice, or speak of that kind-hearted goddess in any terms equal to her merit.

Vulcan gave me a very concise account of Mount Etna; he said it was nothing more than an accumulation of ashes thrown from his forge; that he was frequently obliged to chastise his people, at whom, in his passion he made it a practice to throw red-hot coals. 'Our quarrels,' added he, 'last sometimes three or four months, and these appearances of coals or cinders in the world are what I find you mortals call eruptions.' Mount Vesuvius, he assured me, was another of his shops, to which he had a passage three hundred and fifty leagues under the bed of the sea, where similar quarrels produced similar eruptions. I should have continued here as an humble attendant upon Madam Venus, but some busy tatlers, who delight in mischief, whispered a tale in Vulcan's ear, which roused in him a fit of jealousy not to be appeased. Without the least previous notice he took me one morning under his arm and held me at arm's length over a well with a wide mouth saying: 'Ungrateful mortal, return to the world from whence you came.'

Without giving me the least opportunity of reply, he dropped me in the centre. I found myself descending with an increasing rapidity, till the horror of my mind deprived me of all reflection. I suppose I fell into a trance. From which I was suddenly roused by plunging into a large body of water illuminated by the rays of the sun.

CHAPTER SIXTEEN

As I have related elsewhere, I could, from my infancy swim well and play tricks in the water. I now found myself in paradise, considering the horrors of mind I had just been released from. After looking about me some time, I could discover nothing but an expanse of sea, extending beyond the eye in every direction. I also found it very cold, a different climate from Master Vulcan's workshop. At last I observed at some distance, a body of amazing magnitude like a huge rock, approaching me. I soon discovered it to be a piece of floating ice; I swam round it till I found a place where I could ascend to the top, which I did, but not without some difficulty. Still I was out of sight of land, and despair returned with double force: however, before night came on, I saw a sail, which we approached very fast; when it was within a very small distance I hailed them in German; they answered in Dutch; I then flung myself into the sea, and they threw out a rope, by which I was taken on board. I now inquired where we were, and was informed, in the great Southern Ocean where I had already suffered shipwreck once before. This opened a discovery which removed all my doubts and difficulties. It was now evident that I had passed from Mount Etna through the centre of the earth to the South Seas; this, gentlemen, was a much shorter cut than going round the world, and which no man has accomplished, or ever attempted, but myself: however, the next time I perform it, I will be much more particular in my observations.

I took some refreshment, and went to rest. I found next morning that we were now exactly in Captain Cook's first track, and arrived the next morning in Botany Bay. This place I would by no means recommend to the English government as a receptacle for felons, or place of punishment: it should rather be the reward of merit, nature having most bountifully bestowed her best gifts upon it.

We stayed here but three days; the fourth after our departure a most dreadful storm arose, which in a few hours destroyed all our sails, splintered our bowsprit, and brought down our topmast; it fell directly upon the box that enclosed our compass, which, with the compass, was broken to pieces. Every one who has been at sea knows the consequences of such a misfortune; we now were at a loss where to steer. At length the storm abated, and we began to observe an amazing change in everything about us; our spirits became light, our noses were regaled with the most aromatic effluvia imaginable: the sea had also changed its complexion, and from green became white. Soon after these wonderful alterations we saw land, and not at any great distance an inlet, which we sailed up near sixty leagues, and found it wide and deep, flowing with milk of the most delicious taste. Here we landed, and soon found it was an island consisting of one large cheese: we discovered this by one of the company fainting away as soon as we landed; this man always had an aversion to cheese: when he recovered, he desired the cheese to be taken from under his feet; upon examination we found him perfectly right, for the whole island, as before observed, was nothing but a cheese of immense magnitude! Upon this the inhabitants, who are amazingly numerous, principally sustain themselves, and it grows every night in proportion as it is consumed in the day. Here seemed to be plenty of vines, with bunches of large grapes, which, upon being pressed, yielded nothing but milk. We saw the inhabitants running races upon the surface of the milk; they were upright, comely figures, nine feet high, have three legs, and but one arm; upon the whole, their form was graceful, and when they quarrel, they exercise a straight horn, which grows in adults from the centre of their foreheads, with great adroitness: they did not sink at all, but ran and walked upon the surface of the milk, as we do upon a bowling-green.

Upon this island of cheese grows plenty of corn, the ears of which produce loaves of bread, ready made, of a round form like mushrooms. We discovered, in our rambles over this cheese, seventeen other rivers of milk, and ten of wine.

After thirty-eight days' journey we arrived on the opposite side to that on which we landed; here we found some blue mould, as cheese-eaters call it, from whence spring all kinds of rich fruit: instead of breeding mites it produced peaches, nectarines, apricots, and a thousand delicious fruits, which we are not acquainted with. In these trees, which are of an amazing size, were plenty of birds' nests; amongst others was a kingfisher's of prodigious magnitude; it was at least twice the circumference of the dome of St Paul's Church in London. Upon inspection, this nest was made of huge trees, curiously joined together; there were upwards of five hundred eggs in this nest, and each of them was as large as four common hogsheads or eight barrels, and we could not only see, but hear the young ones chirping within. Having, with great fatigue, cut open one of these eggs, we let out a young one unfeathered, considerably larger than twenty full-grown vultures. Just as we had given this youngster his liberty, the old kingfisher lighted, and seizing our captain, who had been active in breaking the egg, in one of her claws, flew with him above a mile high, and then let him drop into the sea, but not till she had beaten all his teeth out of his mouth with her wings.

Dutchmen generally swim well; he soon joined us, and we retreated to our ship. At once we unmoored, and set sail from this extraordinary country, when, to our astonishment, all the trees upon shore, of which there were a great number very tall and large, paid their respects to us twice, bowing to exact time, and immediately recovered their former posture, which was quite erect.

By what we could learn of this CHEESE, it was considerably larger than the continent of all Europe!

After sailing three months we knew not where, being still without compass, we arrived in a sea which appeared to be almost black; upon tasting it, we found it most excellent wine, and had great difficulty to keep the sailors from getting drunk with it: however, in a few hours we found ourselves surrounded by whales and other animals of an immense magnitude; one of which appeared to be too large for the eye to form a judgment of: we did not see him till we were close to him. This monster drew our ship, with all her masts standing, and sails bent, by suction into its mouth, between its teeth, which were much larger and taller than the mast of a first-rate man-of-war. After we had been in his mouth some time, he opened it pretty wide, took in an immense quantity of water, and floated our vessel, which was at least 500 tons burthen, into his stomach; here we lay as quiet as at anchor in a dead calm. The air, to be sure, was rather warm, and very offensive. We found anchors, cables, boats and barges in abundance, and a considerable number of ships which the creature had swallowed. Everything was transacted by torch-light; no sun, no moon, no planet, to make observations from. We were all generally afloat and aground twice a-day: whenever he drank, it became high water with us; and when he evacuated, we found ourselves aground: upon a moderate computation, he took in more water at a single draught than is generally to be found in the Lake of Geneva, though that is above thirty miles in circumference.

On the second day of our confinement in these regions of darkness, I ventured at low water, as we called it, when the ship was aground, to ramble with the Captain, and a few of the other officers, with lights in our hands: we met with people of all nations, to the amount of upwards of ten thousand; they were going to hold a council how to recover their liberty; some of them having lived in this animal's stomach several years, there were several children here who had never seen the world, their mothers having lain in repeatedly in this warm situation.

Just as the chairman was going to inform us of the business upon which we were assembled, this plaguy fish, becoming thirsty, drank in his usual manner: the water poured in with such impetuosity, that we were all obliged to retreat to our respective ships immediately, or run the risk of being drowned; some were obliged to swim for it, and with difficulty saved their lives. In a few hours after, we were more fortunate; we met again just after the monster had evacuated. I was chosen chairman, and the first thing I did was to propose splicing two main-masts together; and the next time the monster opened his mouth, to be ready to wedge them in, so as to prevent his shutting it. It was unanimously approved. One hundred stout men were chosen upon this service. We had scarcely got our masts properly prepared, when an opportunity offered; the monster opened his mouth, immediately the top of the mast was placed against the roof, and the other end pierced his tongue, which effectually prevented him from shutting his mouth. As soon as everything in his stomach was afloat, we manned a few boats, who rowed themselves and us into the world. The daylight, after, as near as we could judge, three months' confinement in total darkness, cheered our spirits surprisingly. When we had all taken our leave of the capacious animal, we mustered just a fleet of ninety-five ships, of all nations, who had been in this confined situation.

Next, I had to visit St Petersburgh for the second time; here an old friend gave me a most excellent pointer. I had the misfortune to have him shot soon after by a blundering sportsman, who fired at him instead of a covey of partridges which he had just set. Of this creature's skin I have had this waistcoat made which always leads me involuntarily to game if I walk in the fields in the proper season; and when I come within shot, one of the buttons constantly flies off, and lodges upon the spot where the sport is, and as the birds rise, being always primed and cocked, I never miss them. Here are now but three buttons left. I shall have a new set sewed on against the shooting season commences.

When a covey of partridges is disturbed in this manner, by the button falling amongst them, they always rise from the ground in a direct line before each other. I one day, by forgetting to take my ramrod out of my gun, shot it straight through a leash, as regularly as if the cook had spitted them. I had forgot to put in any shot, and the rod had been made so hot with the powder, that the birds were completely roasted by the time I reached home.

Since my arrival in England I have accomplished what I had very much at heart, viz. providing for the inhabitant of the Cheese Island, whom I had brought with me. My old friend, Sir William Chambers, who has designed the new buildings at Somerset House seemed much distressed for a contrivance to light the lamps there. The common mode with ladders, he observed, was both dirty and inconvenient. My native of the Cheese Island popped into my head; he

They could not discover any solution to their problem. (See page 94)

was only nine feet high when I first brought him from his own country, but was now increased to ten and a half: I introduced him to Sir William, and he is now appointed to the honourable office of lamp lighter.

CHAPTER SEVENTEEN

About the beginning of his present Majesty's reign I had some business with a distant relation who then lived on the Isle of Thanet. I made it a practice during my residence there, the weather being fine, to walk out every morning. After a few of these excursions, I observed an object upon a great eminence about three miles distant; I extended my walk to it, and found the ruins of an ancient temple; I walked round it several times, meditating. On the eastern end were the remains of a lofty tower, near forty feet high, overgrown with ivy, the top apparently flat; and I resolved, if possible, to gain the summit; which I at length effected by means of the ivy, though not without great difficulty and danger: the top I found covered with this evergreen, except a large chasm in the middle. Curiosity prompted me to sound the opening in the middle, in order to ascertain its depth, believing that it might probably communicate with some unexplored subterranean cavern in the hill; but having no line, I was at a loss how to proceed.

After revolving the matter in my thoughts for some time, I resolved to drop a stone down and listen to the echo: having found one that answered my purpose, I placed myself over the hole, with one foot on each side, and stooping down to listen, I dropped the stone; which I had no sooner done

than I heard a rustling below, and suddenly a monstrous
eagle put up its head right opposite my face; and rising up
with irresistible force, carried me away seated on its shoulders. I instantly grasped it round the neck, which was large
enough to fill my arms; and its wings, when extended, were
ten yards from one extremity to the other. As it rose with a
regular ascent, my seat was perfectly easy, and I enjoyed the
prospect below with inexpressible pleasure.

It hovered over Margate for some time, was seen by
several people, and many shots were fired at it; one ball hit
the heel of my shoe, but did me no injury. I then directed its
course to Dover cliff, where it alighted, and I thought of dismounting; but was prevented by a sudden discharge of
musquetry from a party of marines that were exercising on
the beach: the balls flew about my head, and rattled on the
feathers of the eagle like hail-stones; yet I could not perceive
it had received any injury. It instantly reascended and flew
over the sea towards Calais; but so very high that the
Channel seemed to be no broader than the Thames at
London Bridge.

In a quarter of an hour I found myself over a thick wood
in France, where the eagle descended very rapidly, which
caused me to slip down to the back part of its head; but
alighting on a large tree, and raising its head, I recovered
my seat as before, but saw no possibility of disengaging
myself without the danger of being killed by the fall: so I
determined to sit fast, thinking it would carry me to the
Alps, or some other high mountain, where I could dismount
without any danger. After resting a few minutes it took
wing, flew several times round the wood, and screamed loud
enough to be heard across the English Channel. In a few
minutes one of the same species arose out of the wood, and
flew directly towards us: it surveyed me with evident marks
of displeasure, and came very near me. After flying several
times round, they both directed their course to the south-

west. I soon observed that the one I rode upon could not keep pace with the other, but inclined towards the earth, on account of my weight. Its companion perceiving this, turned round and placed itself in such a position that the other could rest its head on its rump: in this manner they proceeded till noon, when I saw the rock of Gibraltar very distinctly.

The day being clear, notwithstanding my degree of elevation, the earth's surface appeared just like a map, where land, sea, lakes, rivers, mountains, and the like, were perfectly distinguishable; so I was at no loss to determine what part of the globe I was in.

A few moments later, looking before me with inexpressible pleasure, I observed that the eagles were preparing to light on the peak of Teneriffe: they descended on the top of a rock; but seeing no possible means of escape if I dismounted, determined me to remain where I was. The eagles sat down seemingly fatigued, when the heat of the sun soon caused them both to fall asleep; nor did I long resist its fascinating power. In the cool of the evening, when the sun had retired below the horizon, I was roused from sleep by the eagle moving under me; and having stretched myself along its back, I sat up, and reassumed my travelling position, when they both took wing, and having placed themselves as before, directed their course to South America. The moon shining bright during the whole night, I had a fine view of all the islands in those seas.

About the break of day we reached the great continent of America, that part called Terra Firma, and descended on the top of a very high mountain. At this time the moon, far distant in the west, and obscured by dark clouds, but just afforded light sufficient for me to discover a kind of shrubbery all around, bearing fruit something like cabbages, which the eagles began to feed on very eagerly. I endeavoured to discover my situation, but fogs and passing

clouds involved me in the thickest darkness; and what
rendered the scene still more shocking was the tremendous
howling of wild beasts some of which appeared to be very
near: however, I determined to keep my seat, imagining that
the eagle would carry me away if any of them should make a
hostile attempt. When daylight began to appear, I thought
of examining the fruit which I had seen the eagles eat; and
as some was hanging which I could easily come at, I took out
my knife and cut a slice; but how great was my surprise to
see that it had all the appearance of roast beef regularly
mixed, both fat and lean! I tasted it, and found it well
flavoured and delicious; then cut several large slices and put
them in my pocket, where I found a crust of bread which I
had brought from Margate. I made a hearty meal of bread
and cold beef fruit. I then cut down two of the largest
plants that grew near me, and tying them together with one
of my garters, hung them over the eagle's neck for another
occasion, filling my pockets at the same time. While I was
settling these affairs, I observed a large fruit like an inflated
bladder; and striking my knife into one of them, a fine pure
liquor like Hollands gin gushed out, which the eagles
observing, eagerly drank up from the ground. I cut down the
bladder as fast as I could, and saved about half a pint in the
bottom of it, which I tasted, and could not distinguish it
from the best mountain wine. I drank it all, and found myself
greatly refreshed.

By this time the eagles began to stagger against the
shrubs and soon they were lying on the grass fast asleep,
being intoxicated with the liquor they had drunk. As for me
I found myself considerably elevated by it, and seeing everything quiet, I began to search for some more. Having cut
down two large bladders, about a gallon each, I tied them
together, and hung them over the neck of the other eagle;
and two smaller ones I tied with a cord round my own waist.
Having secured a good stock of provisions, and perceiving

the eagles begin to recover. I again took my seat. In half an hour they arose majestically from the place, without taking the least notice of their incumbrance. Each reassumed its former station; and directing their course to the northward, they crossed the Gulf of Mexico, entered North America, and steered directly for the Polar regions; which gave me the finest opportunity of viewing this vast continent that can possible be imagined.

Before we entered the frigid zone the cold began to affect me; but piercing one of my bladders, I took a draught, and found that it could make no impression on me afterwards. Passing over Hudson's Bay, I saw several of the company's ships lying at anchor, and many tribes of Indians marching with their furs to market.

By this time I was so reconciled to my seat, and become such an expert rider, that I could sit up and look around me; but in general I lay along the eagle's neck, grasping it in my arms, with my hands immersed in its feathers, in order to keep them warm.

In these cold climates I observed that the eagles flew with greater rapidity, in order, I suppose, to keep their blood in circulation. In passing Baffin's Bay I saw several large Greenlandmen to the eastward, and many surprising mountains of ice in those seas.

Having given my eagles plenty to eat and drink, I turned their heads towards the south-east, which course they pursued with a rapid motion. In a few hours I saw the western isles, and soon after had the inexpressible pleasure of seeing Old England. I took no notice of the seas or islands over which I passed.

Recovering a little, I once more looked down upon the earth; when, to my inexpressible joy, I saw Margate at a little distance, and the eagle descending on the old tower whence it had carried me on the morning of the day before. It no sooner came down than I threw myself off, happy to find that I was once more restored to the world. The eagle flew away in a few minutes, and I sat down to compose my fluttering spirits, which I did in a few hours.

I soon paid a visit to my friends, and related these adventures. Amazement stood in every countenance; their congratulations on my returning in safety were repeated with an unaffected degree of pleasure, and we passed the evening as we are doing now, every person present paying the highest compliments to my courage and veracity.

THE MEN OF SCHILDA

THE MEN OF SCHILDA

1 *How it all began*

Long ago and far away, there flourished a small town by the name of Schilda. Its people were called Schildburgers and they were famous far and wide as men of judgment and good sense. Kings and emperors, princes and lords, would order a messenger to ride post haste and bring a Schildburger back to court, whenever some knotty problem of state arose which baffled ministers and counsellors. And when the wise man had delivered his opinion, he would be sent home to Schilda laden with riches and honours, in gratitude for the soundness of his advice.

As time went by, many rulers became dissatisfied with these arrangements. What a business it was having to send for a Schildburger each time there was trouble, and how much better it would be to have a resident Schildburger at court, on hand whenever he was needed. So one by one the men of Schilda were summoned, first to this princeling and then to another, until there was not a grown man left in the little township.

Before long, things had reached a pretty pass. The womenfolk were left entirely on their own in Schilda. They had to manage their households and bring up their children single-handed, and they were left to administer their estates as best they could. In fine, they had to do all the thousand and one tasks that usually fall to the man of the house and things went from bad to worse. Season by season the harvests grew poorer, the cattle sickened, the servants became impertinent, and the children got completely out of hand without the firm guidance of a father. There was no doubt about it. The town of Schilda was going to rack and ruin.

So the women of Schilda decided that it was high time their husbands came home. They wrote them a long letter describing what was happening, and imploring them to return. And just in case pleading was not sufficient, they added a stern warning. Unless the men of Schilda put in an appearance very quickly, they might find that their wives had had to look elsewhere for new husbands, and the front doors of their homes would be slammed in their faces.

When the Schildburgers read this letter, they were not slow to grasp its meaning. They begged urgent leave of their masters and hurried back to Schilda. There they saw for themselves the damage caused by their absence and they agreed unanimously that they must put their own house in order forthwith.

Next morning, on a fine sunlit day, the wise men of Schilda assembled in the market place beneath the linden tree. They talked long and earnestly about the havoc wrought while they were away, and they agreed that it far outweighed the rewards they had received from their masters, so that it would have been much better for everyone if they had remained at home.

'We must not go away again,' said one elderly sage. 'If foreign princes call for our services, we must refuse to go.'

'That will not do,' replied another. 'If we provoke their anger, they might declare war on Schilda. Surely it would be better to go, but to offer such lukewarm and feeble advice that they do not send for us in future.'

'I have a better idea,' said the oldest Schildburger. 'It is because we are steeped in wisdom to the eyebrows that we are continually summoned to faraway places. If we could acquire as great a reputation for foolishness as we have had hitherto for cleverness, no one will send for us any more and we shall be left in peace.'

There followed a lengthy and solemn debate, for it was a hard thing that men of such renown should end their days as fools. But in the end, they were convinced that it would need all their wit and cunning to play the fool well enough to deceive the world at large. Henceforth, they would have to cudgel their brains to devise the strangest, the most ridiculous pranks the world had ever seen. For love of Schilda, its devoted citizens would abandon their tradition of sagacity and shrewdness, and found a race of simpletons and numskulls.

And that was the end of the wisdom of the Schildburgers and the beginning of their folly.

2. *How the Men of Schilda built a town hall*
Now that the Schildburgers were determined to adopt a different way of life, they decided to make a fresh beginning by building themselves a new town hall. Of course, they were still clever enough to know that they would need wood for its construction, although real fools would have started to build without it. So they set off for the forest that lay in a valley on the far side of a hill overlooking the town.

With the master builder in charge, they began by selecting the most suitable trees and felling them to the ground. They trimmed off the branches and stacked them neatly in heaps. Then they turned to the tree trunks that were left. Panting and puffing, straining and sweating, and with many a break for a rest, they dragged the logs up to the top of the hill, and then hauled them down the other side. They worked away with patience and good temper until they got to the last tree trunk of all. This they handled like the rest, pulling and pushing, lifting and hauling, first up one steep hillside

and then down the other. Half way down, however, the log suddenly slipped from their grasp and began to roll steadily downhill entirely of its own accord. At first it moved slowly, but gradually it gathered speed and rolled faster and faster, bumping merrily down the slope until it reached the heap of tree trunks at the foot of the hill, where it duly came to a halt.

This behaviour was watched by the Schildburgers with mouths agape, and they were mightily impressed that the log had shown such intelligence. 'What fools we are!' exclaimed one of them. 'Here we are toiling away to get the trees down the mountainside, and a mere log teaches us that not only could they have done it better by themselves, but that we should have had great sport watching them into the bargain.'

... a race of simpletons and numskulls

'Well, it's never too late,' said another. 'Let us take them back again. We can carry them up to the top of the hill and there give them a push. We shall enjoy ourselves watching them bumping and bouncing gaily down to the bottom. That will surely repay us for our pains.'

The idea delighted the Schildburgers, and if they had sweated and strained before, they had to exert themselves three times as much to get all the timber back to the top of the hill. But carry it they did, every single log, except the one that had rolled down of its own accord, and this they spared because it had behaved with such good sense.

So they pushed and heaved, they pulled and rolled, they carried and dragged, they lifted, tugged and hauled, until everyone was fairly exhausted and had to rest before the fun could begin. Then inch by inch, they manœuvred the trunks to the edge of the slope and gave them a great push. As one by one the logs went tumbling down the hill, the citizens cheered and clapped their hands for joy.

The Schildburgers were very proud of this first test of their foolishness and they returned to the town rejoicing. They made straight for the inn, where they took their seats and proceeded to run up a pretty bill for wine, to be charged to the public purse.

The timber was cut up and planed; stone, sand and lime were delivered, and when everything appeared to be ready, the Schildburgers suddenly realized that they had forgotten to dig the foundations. They ran home to fetch spades, shovels and picks and any other tools they could find, and they dug and shovelled until everyone agreed that the hole was big enough.

But now there lay by the side of the hole a great mound of earth, which was directly in the way of where they wanted to build. 'It must be removed, gentlemen, it must be removed,' said the master builder, but he himself did not know what to do with it. Then one bright young man came up with a

cunning notion. 'We must dig a new hole, and bury all the soil in there.'

This they did, but no sooner had the new hole been dug when, to everyone's bewilderment, there appeared a fresh heap of earth, for which they had to dig yet another hole. And so this went on, until the last mound of soil was so far from the building site that it was no longer in the way and could be left undisturbed.

Now the Schildburgers began building in earnest, and they set about it with such enthusiasm that within a few days they had erected the three outer walls. For as they wanted a very special town hall, they had decided that it should be triangular.

Next they had to put on the roof. This again had to be triangular, following the three corners of the building. The framework was hoisted into position, and it was decided to fix the tiles on the following day. Everyone hurried along to the inn where the landlord had placed the wreath for the topping out ceremony, and he poured out a hearty draught of ale for one and all.

The next morning, the peal of the bell was the signal for the Schildburgers to come out of doors, for before it rang out, no one was allowed to start work. They all came streaming out of their houses and the roofing of the town hall began. The first comers took their place high along the ridge of the roof, others sat astride the rafters, right to the edge. The rest stood in line, one below the other, with a man on every rung of the ladder and those who were crowded off the ladder stretched in a long row, as far as the heap of tiles which had been stacked a stone's throw from the town hall. Thus each tile was passed from hand to hand, from the fellow who lifted it from the heap, to the one who nailed it firmly in its right place.

At last the work was done and they were ready to enter the building. They stepped reverently over the threshold but

. . . *led the pig by the ear before the court.* (*See page 98*)

hardly had they done so when they found to their amazement that it was pitch dark inside. Why, it was so dark, they
could hardly hear each other, let alone see each other. They
grew alarmed and racked their brains to discover the cause
of the trouble, but try as they might, they could not see that
they had forgotten to put in any windows, so all their
pondering was in vain. There was nothing for it but to call
a meeting to discuss the whole affair.

When the day of the meeting came, all the Schildburgers
assembled in the town hall, for the whole community was
concerned. They took their seats, and each man had brought
with him a lighted taper, which he stuck in his hatband.

The worthy citizens had many suggestions as to how the
darkness could be overcome, but there was not one that all
could agree on, for everyone contradicted everyone else.
However, a majority seemed to think that the whole building
would have to be pulled down, and then started afresh.

Then one of the aldermen stood up. He had once been
considered the wisest Schildburger of all, and therefore, he
believed that now he must show he was the most stupid.

'Fellow citizens,' he began. 'Can we not fill sacks with
daylight, as one fills a bucket with water, and so carry the
light indoors? Admittedly, no one has ever done this before,
but if we succeed, we shall be esteemed as great inventors
and praised for our important discovery. And if we fail, it
does not matter. We shall be counted as fools, which is very
welcome for our purpose and useful for our new reputation.'

This proposal pleased the Schildburgers so much that
they decided to carry it out with all possible speed. As soon
as noon had struck, when the sun is at its highest, they all
assembled before the new town hall. Each man had to bring
a vessel or container in which he could catch the light and
carry it indoors. Some of them brought shovels, hoes, or
even pitchforks, to make sure that each sack was properly
filled.

As soon as the clock struck one, all the Schildburgers were at work. Many of them had long sacks, and they allowed the sunshine to pour inside, right down to the bottom. Then they hastily tied up the mouths of the sacks, and as they lifted them, they told themselves how much heavier they were than before. Quickly they dashed into the town hall, untied the sacks and shook out the daylight.

Other Schildburgers used pots and kettles, or any kind of vessel with a lid to it. Some brought wooden tubs and pails, and a few took out window panes in which the sun was mirrored and carried them inside the town hall. One man even fetched a mousetrap to try and catch the light, and everyone behaved as his foolish head bade him.

Thus they went on the livelong day until sunset, rushing back and forth with such energy that they were almost worn out with heat and fatigue. But in spite of all their activity, they achieved nothing at all, and the town hall remained as dark as ever.

'Ah well, it would have been a fine thing if it had succeeded!' was their last word on the subject.

And with that, they went off to the inn, and felt that they were entitled to revive themselves with wine at the communal expense.

3. *How Till Eulenspiegel came to Schilda*

On that fine summer's day when the Schildburgers were endeavouring to carry the daylight into their town hall, a wanderer arrived in their town and no one could have been more welcome. It was Till Eulenspiegel, who was something of a practical joker even then, although he had not yet become the world-famous rogue one can read about today. As Master Till appeared in Schilda shortly after midday and sauntered through the streets, he was surprised to find them deserted, as if the town were uninhabited. But when he came to the market place there was a great deal of activity. The

Schildburgers were rushing hither and thither, absorbed in their efforts to catch the sunlight and fill their sacks with it.

Till stood open-mouthed, watching all the goings on. He racked his brains to try to account for such hustle and bustle, but in vain. The stout Schildburgers did not notice the presence of a stranger, so busy were they with the task in hand, and Till did not dare to stop anyone and ask him what they were doing. He merely shook his head in bewilderment and betook himself to the inn.

When it was evening at last, several Schildburgers also came to the inn to refresh themselves with a cool drink after the day's task. Now Till ventured to ask them why they had been toiling so hard in the sun. One old man answered him: 'Sir, we have been trying to fill sacks with daylight and carry it inside our newly-built town hall, for it is pitch dark inside, as black as night.'

Then Eulenspiegel began to understand not only what had been happening that day in the market place. He also gleaned something about the intelligence of the Schild-burgers. And with a straight face, he asked the old man if they had achieved anything by their efforts.

'Not the slightest,' answered the Schildburger, sadly shaking his head.

'That is because you did not go about things as I should have suggested,' said Till. 'And if you do not despise my good advice, all is not lost even now.'

The people listened and they promised Till a handsome reward if he would give them the benefit of his wisdom. They ordered the innkeeper to entertain Till at the town's expense, so that he was their guest for the night and could drink his fill without putting his hand in his pocket.

Next morning, when the kindly sun again shone down on Schilda, Till Eulenspiegel was led inside the town hall. With a most serious expression on his face he inspected everything thoroughly. Then he ordered a few of the men to climb onto the roof and remove all the tiles. This they did, for Till inspired the Schildburgers with complete confidence.

'Now you have light in your town hall,' said Till, when the last tile was removed. 'And if it should become a nuisance, you can easily get rid of it again.'

When the citizens stepped inside, they found to their astonishment that it was no longer dark but bright. There was great rejoicing in Schilda, and for his excellent advice, Till Eulenspiegel received a generous reward.

The mayor gave a splendid party that same evening, with music, dancing and fireworks, and Master Till was invited too. There he found the most distinguished citizens, the six aldermen, the guildmasters, the magistrates and the justice of the peace, the lawyers, doctors and many others, all with their wives and children, cousins and aunts, and all curious to make the acquaintance of the clever stranger.

When people heard that he was a widely travelled man, they asked him to tell them his strangest adventures. 'Tell us, Master Till,' said the mayor's little granddaughter, 'which is the most beautiful land you have ever seen?'

'The most beautiful country in the world, my dear,' replied Till Eulenspiegel, 'is a land where there is always peace, where there are only masters and no servants, where no one is poor and everyone is rich. There are no doctors because no one is ever ill, there is no fear or need, no cares or worry, no work and no school.'

'Tell us more about it,' said the little girl, clapping her hands for joy. The mayor saw this and he too stepped closer to listen. The child's parents did likewise, until the whole company was gathered about Till Eulenspiegel and so he went on:

'That happy land is never too hot and never too cold. Summer and winter, spring and autumn arrive together, so that when you go into the garden, you can pluck snowdrops, violets, roses, and ripe apples and pears on one and the same day. You can go boating on the lake and skate on it, turn and turn about. The houses are roofed with pancakes, the doors are made of gingerbread, and round every house is a fence made of sausages, all ready to eat. And thirsty mortals have a wonderful time, for the wells, brooks and streams all flow with the finest wine.

'The fishes there are very entertaining. They do not swim deep in the river as they do here, but walk about on the surface of the water. They are already cooked to a turn, and they always stay close to the bank for anyone to catch. You just call, "*Psst, psst!*" and they leap into your hand, so that you don't even need to bend down to get them.

'There are ready roasted pigs running through the streets, with forks and knives stuck in their backs, so you can cut yourself a slice and stick the knife and fork back again. The roads are paved with cheese puffs and meat pasties, and the milestones are cream buns and chocolate cakes, that grow again when you break off a mouthful. And there is a magic fountain of youth in that country, where an ugly old woman can step into the water and emerge as a beautiful young girl of seventeen or eighteen, no older, I assure you.'

'But that is the Land of Make Believe!' cried the mayor's granddaughter. 'Have you really been there, Master Till?'

'Yes indeed I have. I ate my way through the mountain of cake that surrounds it like a wall.'

'And why did you not stay there?' the child persisted.

'Well, there is an odd thing about the Land of Make Believe,' was Till's answer. 'Dunces and numskulls are highly respected there, and those who are so silly and dull that they can do nothing but eat, drink and sleep are made noblemen. The most stupid man of all is made Chancellor of the Exchequer, while the laziest is crowned king.

'Now if you are not content with such a life and begin to weary of it, you are looked on severely by all true Make-Believers, and if you yawn three times, then according to their laws, you are expelled from their land for ever. And that is what happened to me when I had been there barely a week.'

'You shall stay here in Schilda with us,' said the mayor affably, 'and we shall see to it that you do not yawn three times here. It seems to me that you could render this town many outstanding services, and you have made a good beginning today.'

Eulenspiegel bowed his approval, for it would amuse him to discover still more of the Schildburgers' follies. So he was well content to stay, and the very next day he began to render another of his 'outstanding services' to the town of Schilda.

In a certain field, there stood an old wall, which was all that was left of an ancient building. The citizens went to survey it in a body, hoping they could make use of the stones elsewhere.

When they came to the wall, they observed that it was covered with long green grass, and they were vexed to think of it going to waste. They discussed what the grass could be used for, and as usual there were many differing opinions. Some proposed that it should be mowed, but there was no one brave enough to climb the high wall. Others thought that if there were any good marksmen among them, they could shoot it down with arrows—but no one in Schilda possessed a cross-bow.

After a little, Eulenspiegel stepped forward and said that it was not necessary either to mow the grass or shoot it down. Allow the cattle to graze along the wall, and they would soon deal with the plentiful crop, for they are naturally fond of grass.

The whole community agreed with such a good idea, and as the mayor was their leading citizen, it was thought only right and proper that his cow should be the first to benefit. The ordinary cows could take their turn afterwards. The mayor, in the name of his cow, thanked everyone for the honour, and the animal was fetched. A stout rope was placed round her neck, the end of the rope was thrown over the wall and everyone began pulling, using all their combined strength. The noose round the cow's neck grew tighter and tighter, and as the poor beast was being choked, she gasped for breath and her tongue lolled.

The first man to see this cried out with delight: 'Pull, pull, just one more heave will do it!' And the mayor himself exclaimed: 'Look, she can smell the fresh grass. See how she's stretching out her tongue to lick it. What a pity she's too clumsy to help herself. Perhaps some of you should climb up to assist her.'

But no matter how they strove, the Schildburgers could not quite hoist the cow to the top of the wall. When, at last, they had to lower her, they found to their consternation that she was dead. The lush grass was left uneaten on the wall, and everyone felt sorry for the cow that had stretched out her tongue so eagerly for the feast, but had died before she could enjoy it.

Still, one piece of good luck came out of this misfortune. Because the whole town had united to try to help the cow, the carcase provided a fine communal banquet of good roast beef, at which the mayor was host.

4. *The quarrel about the donkey's shadow*

Till Eulenspiegel took lodgings at the house of a Schildburger named Hans Jacob. Now Hans Jacob was an honest donkey driver, but as luck would have it, he was dogged by ill fortune and in the course of one short week, he lost all his three donkeys. This is how it happened.

Hans Jacob decided that his asses deserved a day off, and so he led them out one day to graze in the meadow beyond the town. There they ate their fill and capered about to their hearts' content. When evening came and it grew cool, Hans

Jacob mounted one of the donkeys and, driving the other two before him, he returned to Schilda. As they arrived at the stable, Hans counted his stock, but he could see only the two asses in front of him.

'Thunder and lightning!' he exclaimed. 'Someone has played a trick on me. Where has my third donkey got to? There were certainly three of them this morning.'

He turned round and rode back to the meadow in a hurry, but he was in such haste that he forgot to close the stable door. He reached the meadow and rode up and down, looking behind this bush and that, but without success. The donkey was nowhere to be found.

Meanwhile, night had fallen. Tired and despondent, the unfortunate donkey driver dismounted and stopped for a breather, when behold! there stood the lost donkey before him.

'Oh, my dear donkey, dear little ass,' cried Hans Jacob joyfully, hugging the donkey and stroking it fondly. Then he took it by the halter and led it home. In the meantime, the other two donkeys had found life very dull by themselves, and so they had made their way out of the stable door, through the town gate and into the wide world. And where they went, no one has ever discovered.

When Hans Jacob realized his loss, the donkey he had found again had to bear the brunt of its master's anger, for it was the cause of the disaster. If only it had not lost itself, its two comrades would not have run away. Hans Jacob was so vexed with this donkey that he could not bear the sight of it any longer and the very next day, he sold it to a dealer for ten talers. But as one cannot be a donkey driver without a donkey, Hans Jacob went to the market a few days later to buy himself another one.

Now it happened by chance that Hans Jacob arrived there just as his own donkey was about to be auctioned. The auctioneer led the donkey round in a circle and praised its virtues. 'A strong, grey donkey, sound in wind and limb, and a sturdy ambler.'

'Well, well,' thought Hans Jacob. 'I never knew my donkey was an ambler. Fancy that!' And as at that moment, someone bid ten talers for the donkey, Hans Jacob quickly made up his mind. 'Eleven talers,' he called aloud and then muttered in his beard, 'Why shouldn't I bid for my own donkey, now that they tell me he's an ambler.'

'Eleven and a half talers,' bid another Schildburger.

'Twelve!' cried Hans Jacob in a loud voice, and as there was no higher offer, the auctioneer shouted: 'Twelve talers I am bid. Going, going, gone!' So once again the donkey was Hans Jacob's property and he led it home very pleased with himself.

That evening, a certain Master Breck sent a servant-girl to Hans Jacob's house, to ask if he might hire the donkey for the following day. Master Breck was a quack and he used to visit the country fairs, drawing people's teeth and selling toothpowder, mouthwash, and various potent remedies against sundry disorders.

Hans Jacob agreed, and it was arranged that on the following day, the donkey would carry Master Breck and his pack, to say nothing of his dinner, to a neighbouring village. Hans Jacob was to accompany them and ride the donkey home again that evening.

Early next morning they all set off. The road led across a wide, open moor and as it was high summer, the heat grew oppressive. Master Breck looked round for a shady spot to rest a little, but there was no tree or bush as far as the eye could see, nor any object which offered a little shade. Soon Master Breck could bear the sun's rays no longer, so he stopped, dismounted, and seated himself in the donkey's shadow.

'Now sir,' frowned Hans Jacob, 'what does this mean?'

'Only that I want to sit in the shade for a moment,'

answered the quack. 'The sun is blazing down on the top of my head, and I cannot stand it.'

'No, no, my good sir,' protested Hans Jacob. 'You did not specify that. You hired my donkey, but you did not mention its shadow.'

'You must be joking, my friend,' said Master Breck, laughing. 'The shadow goes with the donkey, that is understood.'

'Nothing of the sort,' retorted Hans Jacob. 'You only hired my donkey. If you wanted the shadow with it, you should have said so in advance. In a word, sir, get up and go on with your journey, or pay me what is due for the shadow.'

'What!' shouted the quack. 'I'd be a threefold ass myself if I did that. The donkey is mine for the day, and I shall sit in its shade whenever I please.'

'In that case,' said Hans Jacob coolly, 'we'll go straight back to Schilda and see the justice of the peace. He shall decide which of us is right. I'd like to see the man who uses my donkey's shadow without my consent.'

What could Master Breck do, since the donkey driver was undoubtedly bigger and stronger than he? He had no option but to return to Schilda.

Master Breck and Hans Jacob appeared together before the worthy justice of the peace, and they were so indignant by now that they both lodged their complaints at one and the same time, protesting at the tops of their voices.

'A remarkable business,' said the magistrate. 'Now begin again and explain what it is all about, but one at a time please, for I cannot make out a word you say when you both shout together.'

'Your honour,' began Master Breck. 'I hired Hans Jacob's donkey for the day. I admit that there was no mention of its shadow, but who has ever heard that you need a special clause about a donkey's shadow in such a contract? After all, this isn't the first donkey to be hired in Schilda.'

'Your honour,' cried Hans Jacob. 'Why should my donkey be made to stand in the sun for nothing, so that someone else can enjoy its shadow? A donkey and its shadow are two different things, and if a man wants to use the shadow, he ought to pay for it.'

'I'll not pay him one farthing more!' shouted the quack.

'And I demand my rights!' cried the donkey driver.

'Where is the donkey?' asked the justice in a sore dilemma.

'It is standing in the street, your honour.'

'Then bring it into the yard.'

So the main character in the drama was led in. The ass pricked its ears, as it looked first at the two gentlemen and then at its master. Then it bared its teeth, let its ears droop and refused to say a word.

The justice did his best to settle the dispute amicably, but there was no healing the breach. In the end, he decided that the matter must go before the court and the hearing was fixed for the following week. Meanwhile, the donkey was to be held in custody, housed in the communal stables.

By now, the story of the quarrel had become known all over Schilda. It roused such passion that the whole town was split into rival parties. 'Are you a Shadow or a Donkey?' they demanded of each other, and it was woe betide the Shadow who had the misfortune to be the only one of his thinking among a group of Donkeys in the street or at the inn. Nor was it any better to be a lone Donkey among hostile Shadows. All in all, it was a bad business, and there was bitter wrangling in the peaceful town of Schilda.

At last the hearing took place in the town hall, with Master Pinch the lawyer appearing for the quack, whilst Till Eulenspiegel himself represented Hans Jacob. Till Eulenspiegel was on his feet, delivering an eloquent speech in favour of his client, when all at once there was a great noise to be heard in the market place below. The hubbub grew louder every moment, and a crowd of people thronged forward, shouting and gesticulating. Suddenly the door of the courtroom was pushed open, and in burst Hans Jacob crying: 'It's gone, it's gone!'

'What's this?' asked the mayor, trembling.

'My poor little donkey has run away,' wept Hans Jacob. 'I went to deck it with ribbons and bring it before this court as a witness, but the keepers who should have tended it left the door open, the villains.'

The keepers, who were of course in court like all the other men of Schilda, defended themselves hotly. 'If we had left the door shut the donkey would not have been able to hear what you were saying up here.'

'Well, thank goodness, he's gone and good riddance,' exclaimed the mayor, greatly relieved. 'Hans Jacob, your donkey could not have done a more sensible thing at this particular moment. The keepers have rendered a great service to our town.' Then turning to the court, he laughed and said: 'Gentlemen, with all our wisdom, we could not have brought the affair to a more fitting conclusion. Why should we rack our brains any longer to find a solution to the case, when the donkey is no longer here? Surely there is no need for us to bicker any longer over the shadow of a missing donkey. I propose that the whole business be declared over and done with and that we should congratulate the keepers on serving the town so well by neglecting to shut the beast up properly. As for you, Hans Jacob, you will receive, at the community's expense, another young donkey, grey in colour and sound in wind and limb, and just as sturdy an ambler as your own donkey was.'

To this wise decision everyone agreed, and the happy event was celebrated with a grand feast.

5. *How Till Eulenspiegel brought light into the town hall at last*
The Schildburgers held many meetings in their new town hall during the summer, and they were fortunate in that it

did not rain at all for many months. Thus they did not really notice the absence of the roof.

At last the sun began to hide its cheerful face and autumn set in with its showers and storms. One day it started to rain unexpectedly during a most important council meeting, and then it was observed only too well that the roof was missing. It became a matter of urgency to put matters to rights.

However, when the roof was retiled and the Schildburgers entered the council chamber, they were dismayed to find that it was as dark as ever it had been before. For the first time, they saw that Till Eulenspiegel had deceived them sadly, and many of them had hard words to say about him. Yet when they were all seated, with lighted tapers stuck in their hats once more, they could not discover any solution to their problem nor decide what ought to be done.

There was nothing for it but to turn to Eulenspiegel again and ask for his advice. 'If you cannot succeed in bringing light into your town hall,' he said, 'why don't you try taking your town hall into the light?'

The Schildburgers stared at him, uncomprehending. So Master Till explained his notion to them.

'You should not have built your beautiful town hall in such a dark corner of the market place. Push it into the light, and then it will be bright inside. Only you must be on your guard not to shift it too far to the other side.'

Everyone murmured their approval and the mayor rose from his seat with dignity. 'Councillors, what Master Till has said seems to me to be both weighty and wise. So as soon as the bell peals tomorrow morning, let us all gather together in front of the town hall, so that we can use our combined strength to push the building into broad daylight. And in order to make it easier to move, let everyone bring a sack of dried peas with him, which we can scatter on the ground. This will help the building to roll along more smoothly.'

The worthy mayor wiped his forehead, for a speech of this

length was a great strain for him. All the councillors praised his sagacity, and nodded their agreement.

Next morning, at the sound of the bell, the Schildburgers assembled. Every man carried a bag of peas on his shoulder, and these were scattered round the town hall. Then when the mayor gave the word, the strongest men placed their shoulders against its wall and pushed against it with all their might. But there were so many peas strewn on the ground that nobody could get a proper footing and they started slithering. And because they were all sliding hither and thither, they thought that it was the town hall moving, so they applied their hands and heads once more, pressing harder than ever against the stone wall.

'That's right, that's right!' the mayor urged them on. 'Now one more try when I give the word. Ready, steady, go!' Alas, they all slipped on the peas and lay sprawling full length on the ground.

They picked themselves up and wiped their bleeding noses, but when they looked at the town hall more closely, it was evident that it still had some way to go. As Till had warned them, however, that they might push the building too far, the mayor placed his hat on the ground to mark the distance needed. He asked Eulenspiegel to stand by, and to call out as soon as the town hall reached the hat.

Then for the third time, the Schildburgers set to work, and pushed and shoved until they were bathed in sweat. Whilst they were thus occupied, Eulenspiegel secretly whisked away the mayor's hat, and hid it inside his jerkin. Then he called out at the top of his voice: 'Stop, stop! You've gone far enough. You've covered the hat completely.'

At this, the stout burghers rejoiced, and they repaired to the inn well content with their success, to fortify themselves with food and drink after such a prodigious effort. But the next council meeting showed that it had all been in vain, for the town hall was as dark as ever before.

When it was clear that Eulenspiegel's advice had led to no improvement, and indeed, the only result of all their efforts had been that the mayor's hat had disappeared, Guildmaster Prim started telling everyone that Master Till was making fools of them all and that he should be run out of town. In the end, the mayor was persuaded that the rogue must be brought to book, and so Till was summoned to the next council meeting.

The mayor addressed the accused, wearing his most solemn expression. 'You are charged, Master Till, with having received a considerable reward from the town coffers on false pretences. You are further accused of being a wicked rascal, who has played tricks on the council and the citizens of Schilda. What have you to say, Master Till?'

'Nothing, your worship,' replied Eulenspiegel jauntily, so that the wise gentlemen gazed at him, puzzled.

The mayor, who was really well-disposed towards Till, could only stutter: 'But your excuse, Master Till? What do you say in your defence?'

'Your worship, wise councillors of the town of Schilda,' said Eulenspiegel, rising to reply. 'You will remember that not long ago you unanimously resolved to abandon your former wisdom, and decided that each of you should hence-forth become a fool to the best of his ability. It has been my task, as a master instructor in folly, to assist you in this faith-fully and truly, in order to preserve your town from ruin. Since I have been here among you, tell me, has ever a prince sent a messenger to seek your advice, or summoned one of you to give him counsel?

'Instead of blame and abuse, then, I deserve much more your praise and gratitude, but as a sign that I am indeed concerned for the welfare of your town, I shall serve you once again in your hour of need and advise you about the lighting of your town hall. Now watch!'

With these words, Till Eulenspiegel stepped towards the

Although the two men lifted the net as high as they could reach, they were unable to catch the moon. (See page 106)

wall of the chamber and, taking a hammer from his jerkin, he struck the wall several powerful blows. There was a loud crack, several lumps of stone fell to the ground, and clear golden sunshine came streaming through the hole into the hall. 'There is your daylight, gentlemen!' cried Eulenspiegel.

At first, the mayor and councillors were dazzled by the light and stared in silence at the bright opening. Then they looked at each other, and one could tell by their faces that they were ashamed of themselves. At last, one man got to his feet and, borrowing Master Till's hammer, he too struck a hole in the wall, close by his head. The others all followed suit, for each of them wanted a window of his own, and soon the wall was full of holes and the chamber was flooded with daylight.

In less than an hour, everyone in Schilda knew that Till had cured the town hall of its greatest disadvantage, and that it was now possible to see inside it. Till Eulenspiegel was the hero of the hour and he was made a Master-in-Lunacy on account of his services to the town.

6. *What the Men of Schilda did to deserve the emperor's charter*

News of the Schildburgers reached the ears of the emperor and he was so amused by their antics that he graciously ordained they might be allowed to continue unimpeded in their folly, and he granted them a charter accordingly. Gradually custom became second nature to them, so that they carried on with their absurdities not out of wisdom, but from pure native foolishness. Everything they thought of, to say nothing of what they did, was now sheer lunacy.

There were among the aldermen two who had heard it said that fair barter is sound business. One evening as they quaffed good wine at the emperor's banquet, they agreed to exchange houses, for such things are likely to happen when wine is in and wit is out. So the next day, Alderman Fry, who lived in the upper part of the town, had his house taken to bits, and carted down piece by piece to the market place where Alderman Groat lived. But the latter did the same with his house, and had it removed piecemeal to the other end of the town. In this way did the two councillors 'exchange' houses, and each was firmly convinced he had made a handsome profit at the other's expense.

Another time, a Schildburger had reared a fine fat pig, which one day wandered into a neighbour's barn and gobbled up most of the oats stored there. The man who had suffered the damage was able to catch the thief red-handed and led the pig by the ear before the court. The court duly tried the case and decreed that the animal must die. The butcher slaughtered the pig there and then, and all its worldly goods, its hog's bristles and pigskin, were declared forfeit according to the law. And since the criminal had met his end as a result of his greed, it was right and proper that the punishment should fit the crime, and that the pig itself should be eaten.

Thus everything was arranged, and to make sure that nothing was wasted, the Schildburgers chopped up the meat, liver, brains and all, and made them into one long sausage, big enough to feed the whole town.

When the day dawned for the sausage to be eaten, the Schildburgers could not find a single pot or pan big enough to cook it in. For they firmly believed that the pot must be as long as the sausage. No one could think what to do, for none of the potters would undertake to manufacture such a large vessel.

In this dilemma, a certain Schildburger happened to be walking down the street when he passed a gaggle of geese. He heard the birds squawking away, saying 'Gobble, gobble, gobble!' But to him it sounded like 'Double, double, double!' 'Stop!' he said to himself. 'Now I have the answer.'

He ran back to the council chamber where there was a meeting in session to discuss this very sausage. 'It is disgraceful, I know, that we must learn from the geese,' he announced, 'but they have just told me that if we double the sausage, we can get it inside a smaller cooking pot.'

When the council heard this, they set to thinking and they agreed eventually that the sausage could not only be doubled but folded over several times. In fact they managed to fold it so many times that at last it fitted in an ordinary saucepan.

When it was ready, the sausage was shared out, and every Schildburger received a piece long enough to go three times round his head. To measure this, each in turn took the end of the sausage between his teeth, the sausage was wound three times round his head, and the piece was cut off. And that was how everyone got his fair share of sausage.

The women of Schilda were no better than their menfolk. They behaved so foolishly that they might have been simpletons all their lives. There was a poor young widow, who owned but one hen, which laid her an egg every day. When the woman had collected thirty eggs, she put them in a basket, placed the basket on her head, and went off down the high-road to sell the eggs in the market place. On the way, she thought to herself how she would spend the money once she had sold the eggs, and she worked it out like this. 'You will get thirty pence for your eggs at the market, and with that you can buy two more hens, so that you have three. They will lay three eggs a day, which makes sixty eggs in twenty days. When you have sold those, you can buy three more hens, and that makes six. They will lay you one hundred and eighty eggs in a month, and you can sell them all and put the money aside. If you keep on saving, you can soon buy some geese, and they will be very profitable with their eggs, goslings, and feathers for down. Before long, you will have enough money to buy a goat, which will give you

milk and kids, and then you must buy a litter of pigs to turn
into bacon and sausages.

'The money you obtain from the pigs will do to buy a
cow, and the cow will provide you with milk, butter and
calves. With the profits from these, you can buy a cornfield,
and then you will need a horse, and farmhands to look after
the livestock and plough the field. In next to no time, you
will have to enlarge your house to lodge all the servants, and
buy more property, for you can't go wrong, you are so lucky
with everything you touch. And then you'll find yourself a
husband and what a fine life you will lead when you are a
rich, proud, lady. Hip, hip, hurrah!'

The young widow was so delighted at the prospect before
her, that she threw her arms in the air and skipped for joy.
Alackaday! there lay the basket of eggs on the ground.
Every single egg was smashed and so were all her daydreams
with them.

Later in the year, the Schildburgers had a mind to build
their own watermill. It was true that no river or stream
flowed through Schilda, but the people thought that if only
they had a proper mill, the other problem would solve itself.
So first of all they climbed a high mountain where there was
a good quarry, in order to cut a big millstone. It was hard
work carrying it down to the valley and it was only when
they got it to the bottom that they remembered how they
had once cut tree trunks to build the town hall, and
had rolled them down the mountainside with very little
effort.

'What fools we are,' said the mayor, 'to have given ourselves such needless trouble. If only we had remembered
about the tree trunks, we could have done the job very
easily.'

So they dragged the stone up the hill again, with the
intention of letting it roll down nicely by itself. They were
about to give it a hearty push, when one of them spoke up.

'But how will we know where it has gone? Who will tell us where it lands?'

'Oh, that is easily taken care of,' answered the mayor. 'One of you must put his head through the hole in the millstone and roll downhill with it.'

This solution pleased them all, and they immediately chose a man who obediently put his head through the hole, and rolled down the mountainside with the millstone. At the foot of the slope, however, lay a deep fishpond and into it rolled the pair of them, the millstone and its guardian. Both sank to the bottom of the pond and none of the Schildburgers knew what had become of them.

Then suspicion fell on the poor fellow who had disappeared. People believed he must have been a thief, who had made off with the stone. So the Schildburgers had the following proclamation sent post haste to all the surrounding towns and villages: Should any person arrive with a millstone round his neck, he must be arrested forthwith, for he had robbed the Schildburgers of their property and should be punished for his crime. But the poor fool lay at the bottom of the pond, too full of water to defend himself and so clear his name.

On the banks of this same fishpond grew a big nut tree, one branch of which stretched out over the water, trailing so low that it almost touched the surface. The Schildburgers saw this, and because they were simple, kindhearted people, they were sorry for the fine old tree. They put their heads together to find out what could be wrong with it, for it leaned out over the water in such a melancholy fashion.

Many opinions were voiced, and at last the mayor spoke. 'Don't be so foolish,' he said. 'Can't you see that the tree stands on dry land and bends over the water because it is thirsty. In my view, the low branch is the tree's beak, with which it tries to drink.'

The others nodded, and they thought that they would be

doing an act of kindness if they helped the tree to quench its thirst. So they tied a long rope round the crown of the tree, placed themselves on the far side of the pond, and then pulled on the rope with all their might. When they had got the branch close to the water, they detailed one man to climb the tree and crawl out along the branch, and give it a final push so that it dipped into the pond.

As the man climbed up and out along the bough, the rope slipped and the tree sprang back with a powerful jerk. Another branch hit the man such a hard blow that it knocked off his head. This dropped into the water and the body fell to the ground.

The Schildburgers were startled when they saw the headless corpse and they asked one another whether or not the man had had his head on when he first climbed the tree, but none of them could say. At last the mayor remembered that he had called out to the man three or four times, but received no answer. So he certainly could not have had his ears with him, and if his ears were not there, probably his whole head was missing too. But he was not absolutely sure, so he suggested they sent to the dead man's wife, to ask if her husband had had his head when he left the house that morning.

'I do not know,' the wife replied, 'but I remember well enough that I brushed his hair for him last Sunday, so he must have had his head then. Since then, I really didn't pay much attention to him or his head, but his old hat is hanging on the wall,' she went on, 'and if his head isn't inside it, he probably took it with him. Or maybe he left it somewhere else. I simply couldn't say.'

The Schildburgers looked inside the hat on the wall, but there was nothing there. In the whole of Schilda there was no one who could say for certain whether the man had left the house that morning with his head on his shoulders or not. Indeed, there were some who maintained that he had never had a head at all. But that is hard to believe.

7. *How the Men of Schilda tried to catch the sun and the moon*

A mile or so to the west of the town but still within the bounds of Schilda, there stood a height known as Acorn Hill. The lower slopes were covered with a fine oak forest and here the Schildburgers used to drive their pigs in the autumn to feed on oakmast. But the woodland covered only the bottom half of the hill, leaving the upper part bare and bleak. The townspeople had tried to cultivate the ground many times with crops of turnips and corn, and Guildmaster Prim had even planted a vineyard on the sunny southern side, but the dry sandy soil defeated every effort. In spite of all their pains, Acorn Hill remained as it was, a desolate wasteland.

Now one fine morning, Guildmaster Prim and his friend, Alderman Fry, came marching down the street and into the town hall where a meeting was being held. With them was Till Eulenspiegel. The mayor greeted the new arrivals and asked them what they wanted. Guildmaster Prim cleared his throat, put on his most important expression, and with all the councillors watching expectantly, he began:

'Most wise mayor, worthy councillors. You all know that Acorn Hill is a dreary wilderness above the forest line, and that such a waste is a great pity. Not a sapling grows there, not even a bush, and it often makes me angry to think how much our town would benefit if the hill could be planted with vines or hops. You know that I myself have spent much money on various attempts, but nothing will thrive there. However, I have been investigating, trying to discover what is wrong, and at last I have found the answer.

'Last evening, Master Till and I went out to my vineyard to gaze at the sunset and to see if it was going to be wet or fine in the morning. As we watched, we saw the sun sinking gradually to rest, directly over Acorn Hill. "Oho," I said. "So you are the culprit. You are the one who scorches our hillside so." For everything was bathed in a fiery glow. The sun did not reply, but let me go on talking, and it disappeared behind the hill like the scoundrel it is. As we were standing there, still watching, the moon rose. "Well now, what do you want?" I asked. "I am sure you are up to some mischief at Acorn Hill as well. Whatever the sun did not burn, you will freeze with your icy rays." And I was right again, for just as I thought, the man in the moon vanished behind the hill and hid his face. "Must you make your way over Acorn Hill every time? Couldn't you go round it once in a while, and sail across the plain instead?" I shouted, but again I got no reply.

'Master Till who saw this with his own eyes too, is my witness. And now, gentlemen, judge for yourselves. Clearly nothing will grow in a place which is subject to the fiercest heat, followed by the iciest cold, that is obvious. What we need to decide here and now is how to put matters right. Let me have your views, gentlemen.'

Alderman Fry spoke first. 'In my opinion, it is better to begin gently. Let us put up a notice on Acorn Hill saying: "Any person, the sun and the man in the moon included, who rides, drives or walks across this mountain will be fined ten talers. Whoever defies this order, will be expelled from the land for ever."'

Another alderman rose to speak. 'When there's a fire, what do you do? You put it out with water. If we fetch pails, ladders and hoses, we can soon put out the sun, you know. And as for the moon, we could blow it up with a couple of barrels of gunpowder. That is what I think.'

'What I suggest,' said Alderman Groat, 'is to fire at these unwelcome visitors with cannons and grenades, and shoot them out of the sky.'

'What do you think, Master Till?' asked the mayor.

Till was enjoying himself as he saw how the seed he had planted in the guildmaster's head the previous evening had taken root and flourished. 'My advice is this,' he said. 'Let us take two long poles, hang a fishing net between them, and carry them in secret to the hill. As soon as the sun and the moon arrive, two men will be ready to lift the staves on high, and so catch both these thieves in the net, where they will be hung.'

This suggestion was acclaimed by them all, but the mayor wondered what they should do with the sun and the moon once they had captured them.

'The answer to that,' replied Till, 'is to have two wooden chests handy, with windows in them and curtains. Then we'll lock the sun and the moon inside these chests, and draw back the sun's curtains during the day, and the moon's at night, so that the whole community can have the use of them still.'

Everyone agreed to this, and it was decided to get to work that very evening.

Three hours before sunset, the mayor blew a blast on a horn, and everyone came running to the market place. They brought with them ladders, hoses, pumps and pails, and a net fixed to two long beanpoles. They found two stout wooden chests to lock up the two intruders, and two pairs of fur gloves to take hold of them and put them in their prisons. Then when everything had been collected, the Schildburgers set out and they arrived in good time at Acorn Hill, for there was still a quarter of an hour before sunset.

Presently the sun arrived. 'Raise the beanpoles, men,' called the mayor. 'The sun is ours—here we have it!'

'No, we haven't. We've caught nothing,' said Hans Jacob, who had been holding one of the poles, for he had stumbled and fallen at the very moment when the sun should have glided into the net. 'Look, it's disappeared from sight behind the mountain.' The two men stood there, empty-handed.

Eulenspiegel assured everyone that it was only bad luck.

His scheme could never have failed, if not for the fact that the mountain had suddenly lurched and sunk. They must not be daunted but should go ahead and try to catch the moon. It could not possibly escape them, and once they had captured it, they could come back next day to fetch the sun.

In order to prevent a similar accident happening again, the Schildburgers fetched chains, ropes, hammers and nails, and they battened down Acorn Hill with stout planks. And this time, they chose their two most important citizens, the mayor and Guildmaster Prim, to hold up the beanpoles.

In due course the moon rose, but it went sailing right over their heads, and although the two men lifted the net as high as they could reach, they were unable to catch the moon. So the second attempt was a failure too.

Till Eulenspiegel, however, had a word of consolation for the Schildburgers. It was only because the mountain had sunk so unexpectedly that their plans had been thwarted. All that was needed now was to build a tower high enough to reach to the moon, and then they could not fail to lay hands on it. But the high cost prevented the Schildburgers from building such a tower, so it has never been erected. In fact, to this very day, the sun and the moon go their ways unhindered over Acorn Hill, and no one can stop them.

8. *How the miller saved the honour of Schilda*

The miller in Schilda was a kindly man, who believed that it was wrong to place too heavy a load on a beast of burden. Therefore, whenever he had to carry a sack of flour from his mill, he used to seat himself on his horse and hoist the sack onto his own back, so as to spare the poor nag.

One day, as the good-hearted miller was out riding in this fashion, he heard two cuckoos singing away in vigorous competition with each other. One cuckoo was perched on a tree on Schildburger land, and soon, this cuckoo began to flag; it could not hold its own against the rival bird, which sang from a tree growing in the next parish, just beyond the Schilda boundary.

The miller saw what was happening, and he was not the man to stand idly by and allow the Schilda cuckoo to be worsted. Determined to go to its aid, he dismounted, threw the sack on one side, and climbed the Schilda cuckoo's tree. There he joined in the contest, and he cuckoo-ed so long and so heartily that at length the alien cuckoo had to acknowledge its defeat, and flew away, humiliated.

Now while this was going on, a hungry wolf stole out of a nearby wood and devoured the miller's horse. The worthy man had no choice but to return home to Schilda on his own two feet.

As soon as he arrived in the market place, the miller told everyone what he had done for the glory and fame of Schilda, and that in so doing, he had suffered a certain loss. For while he was busy challenging and routing the upstart cuckoo, his horse had been eaten by a wolf.

The mayor and the people of Schilda listened sympathetically to the miller's story. They appreciated the gallant way he had defended the honour and renown of Schilda, and they decided not only to replace his horse at public expense, but to make him a freeman of the town in gratitude for his outstanding services.

9. *How the Men of Schilda hid the church bell in the lake*
It happened that a war broke out in a neighbouring country, and the people of Schilda were much afraid that their ancient town might be invaded and plundered. They were particularly concerned for the bell which hung in the church, for the enemy might very well take it away and melt it down for cannon. After long deliberation, the council decided that it would be best to hide the bell at the bottom of the lake, and when the war was over, they could retrieve it and hang it once more in the church belfry.

So the stout burghers lifted down the bell, placed it in a boat, and rowed out to the middle of the lake, where they threw the bell overboard and watched it sink to the bottom. Then one of them had second thoughts. 'But how will we find the bell again, once the war is over?' he asked, puzzled.

'Don't worry your head about that,' said the mayor, and leaning over the side of the boat, he cut a notch at the edge, saying: 'This notch marks the spot, so we can easily find it again.'

Everyone was full of praise for the mayor's great wisdom, and as soon as the war was over, they set out in the boat once more to find the bell and restore it to the town hall. But although they had no difficulty in locating the notch on the boat's side, they failed utterly to discover where the bell lay. Baffled, they could only believe that the enemy must have crept in after all and stolen the bell when their backs were turned. Perhaps a fish informed the foes of Schilda where the bell had been hidden.

10. *How the Men of Schilda bought a mouse-hound and so caused the destruction of Schilda*

For some time, the town of Schilda had been worried by a plague of mice. Cats were unknown there, and soon the mice became such a nuisance that nothing was safe from them. They invaded pantries and larders and ate up everything they could find. No one knew how to get rid of them and the people were greatly perplexed.

One fine morning, a tramp came wandering through the streets, carrying a cat under his arm. He arrived at the inn, where the mice were so tame that they ran about in broad daylight, ignoring human beings.

The landlord asked the man what kind of animal he had with him, and the vagabond replied: 'It is a mouse-hound.' He placed the cat on the floor and let it loose. The cat pounced on the mice, and in the twinkling of an eye, it had killed a dozen or more. When the men at the inn saw this, they asked the tramp if he would sell them the mouse-hound, and they offered him one hundred gulden. The tramp quickly accepted such a lavish sum, and the deal was done. He carried the cat to the town hall where the communal grain was stored, and where there were the greatest number of mice. The cat soon got to work and the townsfolk of Schilda were delighted.

The vagabond, however, thought he had better make off with his money, before the Schildburgers discovered they had paid an enormous amount for a very common animal. So he set off briskly along the high road, in a great hurry to be gone. Meanwhile, the Schildburgers bethought themselves that they would not know how to feed the mouse-hound once it had killed all the mice in the town, so they sent a young man after the vagabond to ask him what the creature ate.

When the tramp saw someone coming in pursuit, he started running faster still, so that the young man could not catch him up and had to ask his question at the top of his voice: 'What does the mouse-hound eat?' he cried. To which the tramp answered: 'Anything you like!' But the distance was so great the young man misheard and thought the other had said: 'Anything alive!'

When he reported this reply to the people of Schilda, they grew greatly alarmed. 'It eats anything alive, you say? Why, what will happen when it has dealt with all the mice? It will attack our cattle, and perhaps us too. We had better kill it, before it devours us all.'

But none of them were brave enough to tackle such a ferocious beast, and the only way out seemed to be to set the town hall on fire, for the cat was still there, feasting on the mice.

And so, reluctantly, for the town hall was their pride and joy, they set the building alight. The cat, however, was too intelligent to be trapped, and escaped by scampering to the roof and jumping from there to the chimney of the nearest house. So the Schildburgers set fire to this house too, so eager were they to see the last of the cat. But the mouse-hound was more than a match for them. As the cat sprang from roof to roof, the Schildburgers set alight one house after another until the whole town was ablaze. When the last house was burning, the cat slid down from the gable and escaped into the woods, never to be seen again.

The Schildburgers looked sadly at the charred ruins of their town, for not a building was left standing. Silently they packed the few belongings that had escaped the blaze, and they set off to find new homes. They wandered far and wide, to the four corners of the earth, settling wherever they could. And that is why you will find the descendants of the Schildburgers in every land, and in every town and village, for surely there is not a place in the world of which it can truthfully be said: 'There are no fools here!'